Finnie Walsh

Finnie Walsh

STEVEN GALLOWAY

Vintage Canada

VINTAGE CANADA EDITION, 2010

Published in Canada by Vintage Canada, a division of Random House of
Canada Limited, Toronto, in 2010. First edition published in Canada by
Raincoast Books, in 2000. Distributed by Random House of Canada
Limited, Toronto.

Vintage Canada with colophon is a registered trademark.

www.randomhouse.ca

Library and Archives Canada Cataloguing in Publication

Galloway, Steven, 1975–
    Finnie Walsh / Steven Galloway.

ISBN 978-0-307-39865-9

    I. Title.

PS8563.A454F56 2010   C813'.6   C2009-904974-0

Book design by Bee Creative

Cover design by Terri Nimmo

Printed and bound in the United States of America

10 9 8 7 6 5 4 3 2 1

for Phyllis, Velma and Tom

Contents

First Period

Finnie Walsh will forever remain in my daily thoughts, not only because of the shocking circumstances of his absurd demise, but because he managed to misunderstand what was truly important even though he was right about almost everything else. Finnie Walsh taught me that those in *need* of redemption are rarely those who *become* redeemed.

Finnie Walsh's parents owned more than half of Portsmouth, the mill town of 30,000 where Finnie and I grew up. I still remember the startled look on my father's face the first time he peered out the front window and saw me in the driveway shooting pucks with his boss' youngest son. My father's concern was not motivated by fear for Finnie's safety; Finnie Walsh, a strawberry-blond, freckled boy with stubby fingers and slate-grey eyes, was not at all frail. He was of a sturdier than average build for a child his age, almost pudgy in a cheerful sort of way, and was only small when compared with his father and three older brothers, who were gigantic.

Mr. Walsh had felt that Finnie would benefit from some toughening up, so instead of sending him to the all-boys' prep school that his brothers and most of the other children of Portsmouth's wealthier citizens attended, Finnie was enrolled in

Portsmouth Public School. It was there, in September of 1980, packed into Mrs. Sweeney's third-grade classroom, that my friendship with Finnie Walsh began.

For four generations, the Walsh family had been Portsmouth's main employer. My father was the most recent in a long line of men named Robert Woodward to work in the Walsh family sawmill. The older I got, the more I understood how much my father wanted me to break the cycle and work somewhere else. With this in mind, my father insisted that I not be named Robert. "Our family," he often said, "is stuck in a rut."

When I met Finnie Walsh, I was too young to realize that we weren't supposed to be friends. It didn't take long for Finnie and me, thrust together in the back row of Mrs. Sweeney's alphabetically ordered classroom, to become inseparable. We each had substantial hockey card collections, although we were at odds about which cards were valuable and which were not.

My favourite player was Wayne Gretzky, who had just begun his second season in the NHL. Finnie's favourite player was Peter Stastny, a Czechoslovakian rookie with the Quebec Nordiques.

"Gretzky's okay, I guess, if you like that sort of thing. I think he's *flashy*," Finnie said.

If there was one thing Finnie Walsh didn't like, it was "flash." It was for this very reason that we ended up playing hockey in my driveway that day instead of the much larger and smoother driveway leading up to the Walsh estate. Finnie agreed that his driveway was in all ways superior to mine; he just didn't want to play there.

The Walsh house was very flashy. It was situated in the middle of a seven-acre lot overlooking the river. Upstream from the mill, of course. The grounds were surrounded by an imposing wrought-iron fence. In many ways the house resembled the American White House, except that it was made of brick. Fountains, benches and a gazebo dotted a magnificently manicured lawn surrounded by an excess abundance of flowers. Mrs. Walsh had been an avid gardener. She had died when Finnie was a baby, but as a tribute to his late wife Mr. Walsh hired an extra gardener to maintain the flowerbeds.

The first time Finnie and I played hockey in my driveway, we didn't even have a net. I drew one on our garage door with chalk and for a while we just passed the ball back and forth, taking the odd shot. My father was working the night shift that week and every time we scored the ball slammed against the garage door and woke him up.

Having had his sleep disturbed several times by a strange echoing thud, my father got out of bed and came to the front window to investigate. He peered between the drapes, watching me stick-handle, feathering a tape-to-tape pass between the legs of an imaginary defenceman. Through the window, I saw him frown and furrow his eyebrows. Finnie took the pass, went inside-out and shot one hard at the top corner. Thud! My father clenched his jaw. Suddenly it dawned on him exactly who had taken the shot. When he realized that Finnie Walsh, Roger Walsh's son, was in our driveway, his eyebrows arched and his jaw unclenched. He disappeared behind the curtains.

Finnie and I celebrated the goal, a perfect combination of teamwork and individual skill. My mother appeared in the window. Her face changed from disbelief to shock as Finnie won the face-off, beating the opposing team's centre, and rifled me a pass. I took the puck on my backhand and, spinning around, gave it back to Finnie. He had gone to the net and was there to tip it by the goalie, who had no chance on the play. My mother vanished into the depths of our house.

Sometime, late in the third period, my mother opened the front door and told me that supper was ready.

"Can Finnie stay?" I asked.

She looked startled, even though I often had friends stay over for supper. "I'm sure Finnie has supper waiting at home for him already, Paul," she said.

"Please?"

My mother hesitated, not wanting to offend Finnie. She didn't know what to make of the situation. "Would your father mind, Finnie?" she said slowly.

"No, Mrs. Woodward. My father usually doesn't get home until late."

"Oh. Well, I suppose it would be all right then."

We went inside. I caught my parents shooting each other questioning looks while my mother set an extra place for Finnie between me and my sister, Louise.

Louise squinted at Finnie; she was always squinting. Louise was two-and-a-half years older than me, a shy kid who didn't really have many friends; she seemed content to keep to herself. She spent most of her time in the basement, where she had an impressive array of toys. Some of them most girls would never have wanted to play with. For that matter, some of them no one would have played with, boy or girl: an old ironing board, a tire jack, a collection of pine cones and duck feathers. What she did with them I never knew. I wasn't much interested in toys then. Whenever I got a new toy for my birthday or Christmas, I would half-heartedly play with it for a few days before it was invariably relegated to the basement, a new fixture in Louise's imaginary world.

Occasionally, when it rained or we were home sick, I would sit on the basement stairs and watch Louise rule her tiny empire. It was understood that I was not welcome to join her, not out of jealousy or spite or sibling rivalry, but because this world was hers and hers alone. She was indifferent to my presence, not ignoring me, but not paying me any special attention either. Louise's "kingdom," as my father jokingly called it, was an interesting but perplexing place.

"Hi, Louise," Finnie said.

She didn't answer him. She looked at the ground, her fingers kneading the tablecloth.

"Louise, be polite," my mother said.

"It's okay, Mrs. Woodward. I understand. Louise is shy."

My father, who apparently was not used to such candour from a seven year old, nearly choked on his coffee. Louise blushed and pulled more frantically at the tablecloth.

We had meatloaf that night, which was never my favourite dish, but since then I have liked it even less. Finnie, however, looked as though he had never eaten meatloaf before and he ate it with such obvious relish that you would have thought it was lobster and caviar instead of ground beef and ketchup.

This impressed my mother immensely. She was not used to people enjoying her meatloaf. "Would you like more, Finnie?" she asked him after he had wolfed down the contents of his plate.

"I sure would, Mrs. Woodward."

"Anyone else?"

"No thanks," my father and I said. Louise said nothing. She wasn't really expected to answer. My mother piled Finnie's plate high with a block of ground beef. My father was pleased; the more meatloaf Finnie ate, the less would wind up in his lunch box. Although he never complained, my father didn't like it when he had to eat the same meal at work as he'd eaten for supper that night.

"Did you boys have a good day at school today?" my father asked us.

"Peter Bartram threw up at recess," I said.

"Has he caught something?" My mother always wanted to know if there was a flu going around.

"No," Finnie said. "Jenny Carlysle kicked him in the balls."

"Peter Bartram is an ass," Louise said.

"Louise!" my mother said, horrified.

We were all shocked. I was shocked that Finnie had gotten away with saying "balls" at the supper table; my parents were shocked that Louise had spoken in front of a non-family member.

"She's right, Mrs. Woodward. Peter Bartram *is* an ass. He beats up kids way smaller than him and he put a firecracker under a dog's collar and lit it."

"He did what?" my father asked.

"He put a firecracker under a dog's collar and lit it!"

"Was the dog hurt?" My mother looked like she was going to cry.

"Not *physically*," Finnie said. "But I don't think it's quite right anymore."

"Why did Jenny kick him?"

"It was her brother's dog," I said.

"If it were my dog, I'd have done worse," my father said.

"If it were *my* dog, I'd have put a firecracker in Peter's pants," Finnie said.

"I'd have put a nuclear bomb in Peter's pants," my father said.

Finnie and my father laughed. He appeared to have forgotten who Finnie's father was. The two of them were talking like they were old friends. Even after my mother cleared away the dishes, they made no move to leave the table. Finally my father looked at the clock and stood up. "Well, I suppose it's about that time." That was what he said whenever he had to go to work.

"What time?" Finnie asked.

"Time to go to work," I said.

"Now?" Finnie apparently did not know that people worked at night.

My mother handed my father his lunch box and he left.

Later, as Finnie was leaving, he thanked me for having him over. "A lot of people don't like me because of my dad."

"Why?" I didn't see why that should have anything to do with it.

"I don't know," Finnie said. "Your dad is nice. He looks awfully tired, though." Finnie stepped out the door and got on his bike. He smiled and rode up the street toward his house.

I closed the door and thought about what he'd said. My father definitely *was* nice. He often looked tired too, that was true, but that evening he'd looked especially tired.

♦

After my father's accident, both Finnie and I suffered great guilt. Finnie took it the hardest, though. He was never quite the same after that; he was always trying to make amends. I suppose it was a turning point in his life. It was my father's accident that turned Finnie Walsh into a goalie.

Without Finnie, I probably would have lost interest in hockey; I really wasn't that good and I knew my family couldn't afford to buy me skates, let alone pay for me to play in the town league. I liked playing on the driveway, but for a long time after the accident it felt wrong. The sound of the tennis ball hitting the garage door gave us the shivers.

"It sounds worse than somebody getting *disembowelled*," Finnie said.

I didn't know what that might sound like, but I imagined it was pretty bad.

There is a difference between someone who plays goal and a goalie; Finnie Walsh was a goalie. He believed it was his mission, his *duty*, to keep pucks out of nets and, in the larger scheme of things, to keep tennis balls from hitting sleeping mill workers' garage doors.

Finnie was my only friend who had real goalie pads. Three days after my father's accident, Mr. Walsh took Finnie and me to the sporting goods store. It was a Sunday, but Mr. Walsh owned the store and could go there whenever he wanted. He told Finnie that he could have any pads he wanted. We looked at menacing black pads, gleaming white pads and lush sable ones, but Finnie was unimpressed. He went to the back of the store and out of the second-hand bin, picked out the most beat-up, world-weary set of dirt-brown pads I had ever seen.

"Why the hell do you want those?" Mr. Walsh asked.

"They have *history*."

I thought that their history, whatever it may have been, did not look very encouraging. "They have holes," I said.

"Holes can be patched," Finnie said and smiled. And so the pads were his. He rummaged through the second-hand bin some more until he found a helmet, pants, a blocker and a chest protector. There were no catching gloves in the bin so he was forced to accept a brand new catcher from his father. It looked out of place, this shiny black glove, next to his beat-up pads and blocker, but it was still by far the best set of goalie equipment owned by any kid around.

Mr. Walsh made me an offer I couldn't refuse. "Tell you what, Paul. You're gonna need yourself a new stick, if you're gonna get anything by Finnie when he's wearing *that* getup."

Looking at Finnie, who had by then donned all of his gear, I was forced to agree with Mr. Walsh. Goalie equipment wasn't as big back then as it is now and though Finnie may have been big for his age, no seven year old is that big. He was so weighted down he could hardly move, but behind his mask he was grinning. He looked huge.

Mr. Walsh was an understanding man, even if he was a little gruff. That was probably one of the few times I ever saw Finnie genuinely appreciate anything his father tried to do for him.

"Thanks, Dad," Finnie said, stumbling across the sporting goods store and hugging his father as best he could.

♦

There was an old reservoir, no longer in use, a 15-minute uphill hike from the Walsh sawmill. There had once been a road leading up there, but since the city had stopped using it the road had been reclaimed by the surrounding forest. Few people ever made the trek, partly because of the lack of a road, but mostly because there was no real reason to go there in the first place.

The reservoir was basically a large hole covered by a flat concrete lid. Beside the reservoir was a decrepit shack that had once been a pumping station. There was also a large pile of gravel, its purpose unknown. Other than that, there was nothing but forest and the faint smell of sawdust coming from the direction of the sawmill.

After leaving the sporting goods store, Mr. Walsh gave me and Finnie a ride to the sawmill and we hiked up the trail that led to the reservoir. Finnie had been wearing his goalie equipment since we left the store, even though it was difficult for him to move and he'd had a lot of trouble getting in and out of the car, let alone up the hill. I had suggested that he carry the equipment in the bag Mr. Walsh had given him, but Finnie had refused.

When we arrived, he stood in the middle of the reservoir and looked around. "What do you think?"

"Of what?"

"Our *practice facility.*"

"It's pretty far to walk just to play hockey," I said, knowing full well that Finnie would walk to the moon before he'd play on my driveway again.

"That's okay. It'll toughen us up."

I, unlike Finnie, was not particularly interested in being toughened up, but it was a good spot. The concrete surface was smooth and flat and there were no garage doors or sleeping fathers around. Eventually we got a net, but that first time we used a couple of beer bottles for posts. I took shots on Finnie and almost always scored. He wasn't bothered by this; he knew he would get better.

"I was really close that time," he would say. "I think I'd get that shot next time."

We played until it was dark, until we could play not a second longer. Finnie was exhausted by his own gear and I was tired of chasing after my shots when they went by him. We were both still reeling from the events of the past few days.

We got back to the sawmill just as the night shift was arriving for work. I saw the startled looks on the faces of the men who had worked with my father; if they hadn't thought it strange that Finnie and I were friends before the accident, they certainly did now. Finnie pretended not to notice and so did I. Mr. Walsh had left for the day, so we had to walk back to town. It wasn't far, but we were tired so we stopped at the school to rest. We were sitting on the swings, not swinging, when our teacher's daughter, Joyce Sweeney, emerged from the bushes behind the playing field. Frank Hawthorne followed her a moment later. Frank was 12 and in grade five, having failed several times. Neither of them saw us. He was certainly not someone Mrs. Sweeney would have chosen to be behind the bushes with her daughter. Everyone, including Finnie and I, thought they knew what went on in those bushes. "That's where people go to do *that*" is what Finnie had told me.

After Joyce and Frank awkwardly parted ways, she walked across the field toward the playground. There she stumbled across two seven year olds, one of whom was wearing goalie equipment.

"Oh!" she said, frightened by our not-at-all-sudden presence.

She smoothed her dress, which was not rumpled. "What are you two doing here?" she asked us.

"Nothing. What're you doing?" Finnie asked.

She could see what we thought she had been doing. We were wrong, of course, but we didn't know that then. "Not what you think."

"What was Frank Hawthorne doing?"

"How should I know? You should just mind your own business. Why are you wearing all that stuff anyway?"

Finnie had apparently forgotten he was still wearing his pads and suddenly became embarrassed. He didn't answer.

Joyce sensed that she had beaten him and turned to me. She must have realized I was an unworthy adversary, however, because she only had kind words. "Sorry about what happened to your dad, Paul."

I appreciated her sentiments, but didn't know what to say. I smiled.

Joyce turned and walked away, then stopped and walked back. "Hey guys, don't say anything to my mom about seeing me here, OK? I mean, I could get into a *lot* of trouble."

"Sure," I said.

"We won't tell, Joyce. Don't worry."

"Thanks." She could tell we were sincere. She didn't know it was because we thought that, if we kept her secret, she might repay us with our own trip into the bushes. Both of us wanted to find out what "that" was all about, although had anyone asked us we would have denied it and said that girls were gross.

After she left, Finnie and I discussed Joyce Sweeney and "that."

"My dad told Patrick that sex is the most overrated thing ever," Finnie said. Patrick, the eldest of Finnie's three older brothers, had just turned 16 and had recently achieved a certain level of fame for his conduct during "career day." When asked by his teacher what he wanted to be when he grew up, he had proudly announced his intention of becoming a porn star. "I'm going to hump my way to the top," he'd told his dumbfounded teacher.

The incident had almost resulted in his expulsion from the Portsmouth Boys' School. Had Mr. Walsh not been the school's most financially generous alumnus, Patrick would almost certainly have been expelled. He'd simply been sent home for the day with a stern warning.

I'm sure Roger Walsh did not have a real problem with his son's aspirations; he no doubt recalled having similar ambitions when he was Patrick's age. He did try to discourage his son though, as he was positive his late wife would not have approved of Patrick's career hopes. Besides, he wanted to shield his son from what was assured disappointment. The life of a porn star is not as glamorous as teenage boys think it is.

As far as I can remember, my father never mentioned whether sex was overrated or not. At least not in my presence. I doubt my mother would have appreciated such a comment. I was only seven, after all, and Louise was Louise. I'm sure it never even occurred to my parents that either of us might require their opinions on the subject. They were right, of course; it was a very long time before I ever got a chance to do "that," and by then I had figured out what I needed to know and wouldn't have wanted to talk to my parents about it anyway. That didn't stop Finnie and me from speculating about the subject though.

"Joyce Sweeney is *hot,*" Finnie said.

I agreed with him. Joyce was definitely a girl to keep an eye on.

Before we could get into any detail regarding exactly why she was worth so much consideration, a car pulled into the school parking lot. It belonged to Mr. Walsh, but it was driven by Patrick Walsh, who had earned his driver's licence only days before. He would have had it a month earlier if he hadn't been grounded for his infamous porn star remarks. Patrick got out of the car and ran toward us. Without saying anything, he tackled Finnie off the swing and started punching him. I was used to this; it was the standard treatment Finnie received from each of his brothers. Patrick was the least severe of the three. He was the largest and the strongest, undoubtedly, but he was secure in his position as top dog and only exercised his power when he thought it necessary. I watched as Patrick pounded his fists into Finnie's padded chest. I didn't want to involve myself in what I considered to be a family affair.

"Goalie pads? You think goalie pads are gonna help you?" he screamed, punching away.

"Fuck off, Pat," Finnie yelled, his arms flailing blindly, hitting nothing but air.

"Who is your king? Who?"

"Fuck you!"

Patrick sat with his knees on Finnie's elbows, pinning his arms. He held Finnie's head still with one hand and extended his middle finger. Finnie struggled wildly, but Patrick was too strong. With his middle finger, Patrick tapped Finnie rapidly and steadily in the middle of his forehead. After several minutes of this, Finnie broke. He could take the punches, but he hated this particular brand of indignity. "You're the king!" he cried.

"Who? Who is the king?"

"You are!"

"Say the oath!"

Finnie started to fight, but the tapping resumed and once again Finnie broke. "Long live King Patrick!"

This was not good enough. "The whole thing!"

"The king is dead. Long live King Patrick. God save the king!"

Patrick got up off a flustered Finnie, acting as if nothing had happened. He calmly lit a cigarette and took a tentative drag.

"Why the hell is he wearing all that stuff?" he asked me.

"We were playing hockey," I answered.

"Dad's pissed that you're not home yet," he said to Finnie. "He sent me to find you."

"We were on our way home."

"Whatever. Come on, get in the car. I got better things to do than chase you around." He turned to me. "You want a ride?"

"No thanks."

Finnie walked to the car. "See you tomorrow," he said over his shoulder.

◆

I didn't see him the next day, though. It was a Monday, but my mother let Louise and I stay home from school on account of the accident. I spent the day silently observing Louise's kingdom and the steady stream of people who came and went, leaving food and cards and other gifts they thought were appropriate. Finnie did not come by, believing that he was not welcome.

We were not allowed to go see my father. It was not considered suitable for children to witness such things. I didn't understand why, so I asked Louise what the big deal was.

"Mom says kids shouldn't have to see stuff like that," she said.

"But I want to."

"Too bad."

Determined to find out more about what had happened, I snuck out the basement window and headed across town, past Finnie's house and past the school. I knew where the accident had taken place, so I headed up the gravel road that led to the sawmill. The sound of machinery permeated the air and the smell of freshly cut wood was overpowering. I had never been inside the mill before, but sometimes, if my mother needed the car, she would drive my father to work, so I knew the entrance.

I tried the door and it was unlocked. It was just past four o'clock; the afternoon shift would be off in a few hours. Inside there was a short hallway with a flight of stairs and a door at one end. The hallway was a depressing shade of grey, the paint peeling off in places. I walked to the end of the hallway and stood, trying to decide whether to open the door or to go up the stairs. Then the door opened and Roger Walsh stepped on my foot.

"Paul! What are you doing here?"

I didn't answer him. I looked down at my feet, sensing I was about to be in big trouble.

"You shouldn't be here. I'll give you a ride home."

"I want to see the mill," I said.

Mr. Walsh paused. "Why?"

"I don't know."

"You want to see where it happened."

"Yes."

He paused for a moment, then held out his hand, which I took. We went through the door and onto the mill production floor. My father worked near the rear of the mill. After the bark was removed from the logs, they were run through a saw that cut the raw logs into various sizes of board. Then the individual boards were cut to uniform length. This was my father's job.

On the night of the accident, my father had been cutting 2 x 6s into 12-foot lengths when, just for an instant, his attention wandered. He was on his fourth consecutive night shift and had gotten hardly any sleep that day thanks to Finnie and me. At three o'clock in the morning, his mind was not where it should have been. He nodded off for a millisecond. He experienced a false sensation of falling as he jolted awake. When he attempted to steady himself, he inadvertently stuck his arm in the path of the blade, severing it just below the elbow.

They rushed him to the hospital and although he lost a lot

of blood he survived. He would be eligible for a disability pension, but we had just been scraping by as it was and the pension was less than his salary. It would take a long time for my father to get used to the absence of his arm; I would often see him absent-mindedly reaching for things with it, surprised when he failed to grasp anything but air.

After I had seen all I wanted to see, Mr. Walsh drove **me** home. I thought for a moment he was going to come in, but he didn't. "Don't worry about your father, Paul," he said. "The fore-man tells me he's a hard worker. Hard workers always end up aces."

I did not believe that then, and I do not believe that now, but I thanked him anyway and went inside. No one had noticed I was gone.

◆

My father returned from the hospital in the middle of October, three weeks after he lost his arm. That was how the accident was referred to around the house: "When Father lost his arm."

At first my father acted as if he had actually *lost* his arm. Perhaps he had left it in the washroom, or in the kitchen behind the refrigerator, or it might have fallen under the seat of the car. I would often see him wandering around the house aimlessly, as if he was hoping to stumble across it. I didn't know what to do; I felt awful about what had happened and more than a little guilty. I wanted him to have his arm back, I wanted to take back the shots that had hit the garage door and kept him awake and I wanted to tell him how sorry I was, but none of these things seemed possible.

I was relieved when he began to seem more like his old self again. On Halloween he decided that he would greet the trick-or-treaters at the door wearing a pirate costume. Louise and I were disappointed when we found out that he wouldn't be able to wear a hook; his stump had not yet sufficiently healed to support any sort of prosthetic device. He assured us that he would make up for this by fully embracing all other aspects of piratehood, including an eye patch and a surly attitude. We waited eagerly that night for the trick-or-treaters to arrive; Louise and I had decided to forgo our own trick-or-treating in favour of watching our father and we were not let down. His performance was nothing less than mortifying, so frightening that it sent several children, screaming, back to their waiting parents before any candy could be procured. One small boy became so distraught that he actually wet his pants and had to be taken home by his mother. She saw my father's act from the curb and thought that he had gone too far. My father scared so many children that it wasn't long before word got out that our house was to be avoided at all costs. As a result, there was plenty of candy left for me and Louise.

By mid-November, I noticed my father was acting even more strangely. He had never had so much free time on his hands, so to speak, and he spent a lot of it sitting on the back deck, thinking. My mother got a job as a secretary in a lawyer's office downtown so, from the time he woke up in the morning until the time she got home, my father completed whatever domestic work he could manage and then for the rest of the day he just *thought*. This changed him, I believe, even more than the loss of his arm.

One day near the end of November I came home early from school. I had not had a good day and felt a little ill, but mostly I was just discouraged. I was having trouble with math and no matter how hard I tried I couldn't seem to understand the problems in my textbook. Finnie wasn't any better than I was; actually, he was a poorer student, but it didn't bother him the way it did me. I think it was because, in Finnie's case, his poor grades were the result of a lack of effort, whereas mine were the result of limited intelligence.

When I got home, my father was out on the back deck. He heard the front door slam and, knowing it was too early for me to be home, came to investigate. He saw me just as I kicked off my shoe considerably harder than I had meant to. It flew across the hallway and smacked against the wall, leaving a dark smear on the wallpaper.

"Paul!" he scolded.

"Sorry," I said sheepishly. Frustrated with the day's events and mad at myself for just about everything, I started to cry.

"Follow me." His voice was stern. My father was a tall, thin man with a leathery face and a receding hairline and, although he was not physically imposing, he had recently developed a certain quiet intensity that I had not yet become accustomed to.

As he led me through the house and out the back door, I thought that maybe I was in for a spanking. My father hadn't spanked me more than a couple of times before he lost his arm, but Louise and I had secretly speculated that one possible benefit of his disability might be that he could do so even less now. He hadn't so much as raised his voice to me since the accident.

My father had me sit in one of the folding chairs set out on the deck. He sat down beside me, retrieving something from his pocket and placing it in my hand. "Here, hold this. You'll feel better."

That was all he said. For the better part of an hour after that he remained silent, staring out at our tiny yard, occasionally lighting a cigarette or taking a sip of orange pekoe tea, which he had recently taken to drinking instead of coffee.

He had given me a rock, a very ordinary rock, special in no way that I could see. I sat there looking at the rock, trying to figure out why the hell my father had given it to me. I was just about to ask him when he stood up and ground his cigarette under his heel.

"Guess I'd better start supper."

Later I told Finnie what had happened and showed him the rock. He turned it over in his hands, shaking his head. "Your father is a very smart man," he said.

"What? I don't get it. It's just a rock."

"Exactly."

I didn't understand what Finnie meant any more than I understood why my father had given it to me. My father gave me a great many more rocks over the years, but it wasn't until much later that I understood why.

◆

It was nearly Christmas before I could convince Finnie to come to my house again. He hadn't been there since the night of the accident, three months earlier. Finnie had great respect for my father. Unlike me, and nearly everyone else, he understood my father almost instantly. In some bizarre way, Finnie was envious of my family. We were, he imagined, *normal*.

There was snow on the ground when we tramped into the backyard and, even though it was well below freezing, my father was sitting out on the deck. He looked up at us and waved, accidentally, with his missing hand. "Afternoon, boys."

"Hi, Dad."

"Hello, Mr. Woodward." Finnie was shaking from cold or fear. He tugged down on the ear flaps of his furry winter cap.

"I haven't seen you around for a while," my father said, smiling.

"No, sir."

"Come here for a moment, would you, Finnie?"

Finnie blanched. He looked at me, wondering if my father was about to exact revenge. I shrugged; I hadn't the slightest idea what my father was up to.

"You come here too, Paul." Now it was my turn to be nervous. Maybe my father was going to cut off our arms.

Slowly Finnie and I worked our way across the yard and onto the deck. We sat down beside my father, who was well dressed against the cold.

"Why aren't you boys playing hockey today?" he asked.

"Well, um, we don't much feel like it anymore, sir," Finnie said. This was a lie; Finnie and I had been playing at the reservoir nearly every day after school.

"Paul, have I ever told you why we named you Paul?" He had, and he knew that he had; this was for Finnie's benefit.

"Yes," I said.

"Then you can tell Finnie."

"I was born on the day that Paul Henderson scored the winning goal to beat the Soviet Union in the 1972 Super Series."

Finnie's eyes widened. "Really?"

"Really," my father said. "Now, I know that you boys like to play hockey. And I know that our driveway's a fine place to play. So if you want to play hockey on the driveway, then go ahead. Just mind that you don't hit the car."

I was relieved; we could keep our arms and what was more we wouldn't have to hike all the way to the reservoir to play anymore.

Finnie appeared unconvinced, however. My father saw this and reached into his pocket. He handed Finnie a rock. "Hold onto this. You'll feel better."

Whatever doubt had existed in Finnie's mind now disappeared. My father saw that Finnie understood how the rock worked, but it didn't matter. They had connected. He never gave Finnie another rock. I guess he didn't have to.

◆

We resumed play in the driveway, with some minor adjustments. We placed our net at the street end of the driveway. Occasionally

Louise would venture away from her kingdom to watch us. She displayed no interest whatsoever in actually playing, even though I was almost desperate to have someone to pass to, but she would watch me take shots on Finnie for hours, carefully observing our technique and once in a while even offering advice. "Your glove side is weak, Finnie." She was right too. He had never liked his catcher; it was "too flashy." He refused to look at the glove while he played, so he hadn't developed any sort of *relationship* with it, which is an absolute necessity for a goalie.

I confess I didn't give him much practice. I knew that I could score on his glove side at will, but the truth of the matter is that I didn't really want to score, ever. Every time I scored, I heard, in my head, the horrible sound of a ball hitting the garage door. I did my best to take shots that I thought Finnie could stop, but not such easy ones that he would suspect I wasn't trying. I'm not sure if he knew or not. If he did, he never said a word.

On rare occasions we would play at the schoolyard with Finnie's older brothers and their friends. Usually Frank Hawthorne played goal, but he was grounded a lot, so sometimes they substituted Finnie. None of the other kids had goalie equipment and neither Frank nor Finnie was willing to loan his out. I was invited because Finnie refused to play unless I did.

They were absolutely brutal games and if I hadn't been so bored with just playing against Finnie, I probably wouldn't have gone. I did go, though, and tried my best not to make a fool of myself when the older boys whizzed slapshots at the net, more interested in seeing if they could kill or maim Finnie than in scoring. Every so often, Finnie would stop a shot with some particularly vulnerable part of his anatomy and it would take him a while to get back up, but he never let them see how much it hurt and he certainly never stopped playing on account of injury.

They didn't play a full rink in the schoolyard. Because of a shortage of space and people, they played four to a side with one goalie. When the defending team got the ball, they had to clear it past a centre line, then bring it back toward the goal. This made it possible to play with fewer people and less running. Because I was younger and less skilful than the older kids, I was never picked for a team. I just stayed in front of the net, perpetually on defence, doing my best to protect Finnie. I ended up blocking a lot of shots myself, accidentally, and once I got hit so hard in the stomach that I actually threw up. As soon as I was finished retching my guts out, I got back out there though, because if Finnie wasn't going to break, then neither was I. This was an attitude that would resurface time and time again as we grew up; without Finnie, I probably wouldn't have had the courage to do half of the things I did.

There was no such thing as a penalty in these games. Kirby Walsh, the youngest of Finnie's three older brothers, was by far the chippiest and meanest player of the group. His favourite trick was to come at you from behind, put his stick between your legs and then pull back, sending the blade into your crotch. He called this "harpooning the whale." "Watch out for Ahab," he'd cry just before yanking his stick back. Apparently he had read *Moby Dick* at the Portsmouth Boys' School. I rather suspect, because of what happens to Ahab at the end and because of the type of boy that Kirby Walsh was, that he read only the first part of the book. Probably never got much past "Call me Ishmael."

It did not take many harpoonings before I learned to be aware of more than what was directly in front of me. It was necessary to develop a sort of sixth sense. Watching out for Ahab was also useful in other areas of defensive play; I was able to anticipate plays before they unfolded and had a much better chance of breaking them up.

Gerry Walsh, older than Finnie and Kirby but younger than Patrick, was one of the best stickhandlers I would ever encounter. He was able to move the ball around on his stick with extraordinary precision and was the first person I ever played against who used his feet to manoeuvre the ball, dropping it back and kicking it up onto his stick at will. He played cheaply when he didn't have the puck; although he never "harpooned the whale," he was fond of using his elbows and wouldn't hesitate to trip you from behind. Once, when I was wearing a hooded sweatshirt, he hooked the hood with his stick and clotheslined me, which hurt like hell.

Jim Stockdale was a terrific passer, accurate to within inches. He couldn't shoot though, and he couldn't take a pass very well. He was easy to cover because you always knew exactly what he was going to do, but he was just so damn good with his passes that there was no stopping them. I won't even get into Patrick Walsh's slapshot; it just plain hurt.

One day, over Christmas holidays, just before the end of 1980, Finnie and I were playing in my driveway, not having been asked to play in the schoolyard. I took a shot, beat Finnie on the short side, winced, and looked up to see Joyce Sweeney standing beside me.

"Hey Joyce," Finnie said.

"Hey guys. What's up?"

"A little hockey. You want to watch?"

I almost choked. How did Finnie expect me to play with Joyce Sweeney, *the hottest girl we knew,* watching us? Besides, I imagined that if Frank Hawthorne found out we were talking to Joyce he'd kick the living crap out of us.

"No," Joyce said. "I'd like to play, though."

This was clearly not what Finnie had in mind, but I was so in awe of her that if she'd said she was going to cut out my small intestine and fly a kite from it I would have readily agreed. I went into the garage and got my old stick.

"Which way do you shoot?" I asked her.

"I don't know." She grabbed the stick and took an imaginary shot. "This feels about right."

Joyce took the ball out of the net and shot it hard against the garage door. Finnie and I both cringed and I swear that I heard the sound of a tea cup being dropped out on the back deck. The ball rolled back to her and she turned and snapped a wrist shot past Finnie and into the net. Finnie didn't even move.

"What's wrong with *you*?" she said, poking his pads with her stick.

"Nothing," he said. "I just wasn't ready."

Finnie hooked the ball out of the net with his stick and shovelled it over to her. She slammed a good, hard pass at me, which rolled off my stick and onto the snow-covered lawn. I realized that it had been a heck of a long time since anyone had passed to me. I got the ball off the lawn and sent it back to Joyce, who shot it and beat Finnie between the legs.

"You were ready that time, Finnie." She raised her stick in celebration.

Finnie shrugged. If you can't beat 'em, join 'em. She was definitely a hell of a lot better than either of us. She wasn't as mean as the kids from the schoolyard either. We played with her for about an hour, then she planted her stick in the snowbank and headed home.

"Thanks for the game, guys."

"No problem, Joyce. You're pretty good, you know," Finnie said.

"It's not a very hard game," she said.

I was shocked; I thought it was plenty hard.

"You want to play again sometime?" Finnie asked.

"It's nice to have someone to pass to," I said truthfully.

"I don't think so. It doesn't much interest me, to tell you the truth."

That was the first indication I'd ever had that there were people in the world who *didn't* like hockey.

♦

The summer of 1981 came quickly. Finnie and I graduated from Mrs. Sweeney's third-grade class. For the next two months we were free to spend our time as we wished. Many changes were afoot, the most significant of which, the one that to this day strikes me as an omen of what was to come, occurred in my father.

Before the accident, my father was known as a steady, good-natured man who was not prone to bouts of inexplicable activity. Following the untimely departure of his arm, however, he began to act unpredictably, even eccentrically.

In early July, my father became very concerned with the state of the garage. He thought, perhaps with good cause, that the items in various boxes and on multiple shelves in some way threatened the family's existence. He spent many hours on the back deck devising a plan intended to systematically eradicate this threat. It was made clear to Louise and me that he was not to be disturbed, even though he was making a great deal of noise, shouting and whooping and banging his fist on the arm of his chair to accentuate some particularly significant aspect of his scheme. Several days after he first announced his intention to save us from the garage, I returned home from the reservoir with Finnie and found the driveway littered with its former contents. I hesitantly ventured past the clutter.

My father had removed, without exception, every item from the garage. The shelves had been ripped out, leaving only three bare walls, a ceiling and a floor. He had then painted the entire room, from top to bottom, a glossy white. He was on the fifth coat when he looked up. He nodded, dipped his brush in a nearly empty can and continued.

The next day, he installed new shelves. Actually they looked more like cages than shelves. The walls of the cages were framed with 2 x 4s into squares about two feet wide and tall. The squares were enclosed by chicken wire and had doors that could be latched shut with a series of hooks. The wire was painted alternately red and black in a checkerboard pattern.

The day after that, my father took a total of 15 empty mayonnaise jars, cut out the bottoms of 14 of them and sealed them together with silicone, one on top of the other, until he had one very tall tube of glass. He cleaned off all the labels, put a spout in the bottom jar for drainage and attached a female hose end to the top jar. The tube was placed in the middle of the garage, reaching from the floor to the ceiling without more than two or three inches to spare. The hose was screwed into the top jar and the tube was filled with water.

I should mention that my father did all this with only one arm. He was extremely resourceful, his determination to complete the job overpowering his physical disability. My father had always been stubborn, but this was different. I was amazed and a little frightened.

Four days after he started fighting with the garage, my father spent the day in a pet store examining goldfish. After six hours, having bothered the store's employees to no small degree, he purchased 25 goldfish. The fish were not gold, as their name suggests, but light blue, with enormous bulging eyes. Perched atop the stepladder, he stuffed them through the tiny gap and into the tube of mayonnaise jars, one by one. Their purpose, he announced, was to keep an eye, or 50, on the clutter.

It took him two more days to move everything back into the garage. Anything that could not be contained in one of the cages was discarded. Certain things, things that somehow offended my father, were also thrown away: the hedge-pruning shears, a gasoline canister, a large Phillips screwdriver and a life jacket. My father developed a classification system for the caged objects that, as far as I could see, was without logic. Anything related to cutting the lawn went into the bottom row of cages, but sharp objects were not placed next to each other. Old shoes were put into two separate cages: left shoes in one and right shoes in the other. The exception were shoes without laces. If a shoe did not have laces, such as sandals or gumboots or old slippers, then the left laceless shoe would be put in with the right laced shoes and the right laceless shoe would go in with the left laced shoes. Of course, this exception had an exception. Where shoes with Velcro were concerned, the two shoes were Velcroed together and placed in with the raincoats. One would think that a one-armed man would have a lot more respect for the wonders of Velcro, but my father hated the stuff.

He alone understood his system. Throughout the years that we lived in that house, no one else in my family was ever known to successfully find anything in that garage. Louise refused to even enter it and my mother went into it only under the most dire of circumstances. Whenever something was needed from the cages, my father had to be recruited to the task.

Finnie, who had a strange affinity with my father's peculiarities, was the only other person who appreciated the garage's hidden science. It took him a while, but if he stood there and thought about it hard enough, he could always find what he was looking for. When presented with the challenge, he would stand behind the mayonnaise jars and place both his hands on top of his head, interlocking his fingers and extending his elbows sideways. He would glare at the cages as if he was staring down a fierce dog. Eventually, usually after about 15 minutes, but sometimes longer, he would walk toward the cages and point at one. If it was one that was up high, he would scurry up the face of another cage to open it. Having found what he was looking for, he would remove the object, close the door and drop to the floor. It once took him two hours to locate a bicycle-tire pump, but he never opened more than one cage.

He couldn't explain how he knew where things were. "It's just a *feeling,*" he said. "It sort of all makes sense, if you just give it a chance."

"*How* does it make sense?" I asked.

"I can't explain it. It just does."

Predicting the whereabouts of objects was not an uncommon occurrence for Finnie. When we played hockey, there were times when he moved to make a save before he could have known that the puck would be shot in that direction. I suppose it is possible that he somehow read the play, that it was just a lucky guess. I don't think so, though.

He knew why Louise wouldn't go into the garage, for example, although in hindsight I guess it was pretty obvious. My mother and I had assumed that it was because she was frustrated by not being able to find anything. Louise didn't deal well with frustration. If something was giving her grief, she'd just walk away from it, forever, and find a way to live without it.

"It's those fish," he said when the subject came up.

When my father designed the fish habitat, or the fish tube, as Finnie called it, he intended to give the fish an unobstructed view of the cages. But he committed two critical errors. The first was making the tube tall and narrow. My father didn't foresee that with such a small surface area at the top of the tube there would not be enough oxygen transferring into the water to keep the fish alive. As a result, all 25 of the fish were dead within two weeks. The second design flaw was that, since my father glued the bottom mayonnaise jar to the floor of the garage, there was no way to remove the dead fish. Every month my father would drain the water out through the spout in the bottom jar and put in 25 new fish. The new fish would eat the partially decayed bodies of their predecessors and then the cycle would repeat itself. My mother and I thought it was a little weird, but Finnie recognized that Louise made more of it than that. It horrified her.

♦

That season, a young Wayne Gretzky scored 55 goals and had 109 assists for a league-leading 164 points. Peter Stastny had 39 goals and 70 assists, his point total of 109 far shy of Gretzky's. It was Stastny's rookie year, however, and he was rewarded for his efforts, winning the Calder trophy, presented to the league's most valuable freshman player. It was a record number of points for a rookie.

Gretzky never won the Calder trophy because he had played for Indianapolis in the World Hockey Association before coming into the NHL and because the WHA was a professional league, he was not considered a rookie when he entered the NHL. In his first two years, however, he broke scoring and assist records held by Phil Esposito and Bobby Orr.

Despite Gretzky's point totals, broken records and exciting play, Finnie remained unimpressed. "Too flashy," he said.

"What about Stastny? He got a whole bunch of points and you still like him."

"He has to *work* for his points."

Where hard work was concerned, Finnie knew what he was talking about. His skills as a goalie were limited; he was slow and he still had a weak glove side. Stout, almost cherubic, Finnie was on the verge of being overweight; although his size helped him to fill up the net, it did little for his speed. He wore his goalie equipment nearly constantly, even though it must have been unbearably hot. By the middle of July, he had passed out from heat exhaustion twice, but it didn't deter him. He knew that he needed to be fast and the only way he could do that was to lose some weight.

Occasionally, when we were allowed to play with Finnie's brothers and their friends in the schoolyard, we would see Joyce Sweeney. We had worried that, since we were no longer in her mother's class, she would stop being nice to us, but she was the same as ever.

One day, we were invited to play in one of those brutal school-yard games. Frank Hawthorne's family had taken him on vacation, leaving a spot open in the net, but as usual Finnie refused to play unless I could too. The crowd consisted of the Walsh brothers, Jim Stockdale and Jordi Svenson, who was big and mean but played cleanly, more or less. A freckle-faced kid named Bruce Selby also joined in. We had never played with him before, so I wasn't sure what to expect.

I was playing well that day. Patrick Walsh was teamed with Jim Stockdale and Bruce Selby. Stockdale could pass like nobody's business and Pat's shot was blistering. Selby turned out to be a decent all-round player, but he was a particularly good checker. There was no way to stop them.

The other team, which consisted of Kirby and Gerry Walsh and Jordi Svenson, was not particularly skilled in any area of the game. Gerry could stickhandle, sure, but with no one to pass to he was forced to take the shot himself most of the time and it was hard to beat Finnie on a clear shot. Jordi wasn't bad, but he was slow and easy to cover. As usual, I was perpetually stuck on defence.

After 15 or 20 minutes, it became apparent that Kirby Walsh's team was severely outmatched. Finnie suggested that we redo the teams, but Kirby wasn't about to admit defeat and responded by cuffing him on the side of the head with his stick. Finnie tried to slash him, but Kirby was too quick. Finnie's stick met empty space, the force of his swing spinning him around and causing him to fall to his knees. Gerry Walsh increased Finnie's humiliation by firing the ball squarely at Finnie's rear end. It made a loud slap as it bounced off him and into the net.

The game resumed and after several minutes Kirby came in on net. I let the ball go by me and as Kirby passed on the left I bent low in the knees and put my hip into him, knocking him off his feet. He landed hard and got up slowly. I thought he was going to throttle me, but instead he sneered menacingly and pointed his stick in my direction, shaking his head.

Since being hit in the ass with the ball, Finnie had been playing brilliantly. It may have been the best game I ever saw him play. He was in place well before the shot, making saves that by all accounts he shouldn't have been able to make. Even his glove was hot. Over the next hour, he let in only a couple of goals and not once did he allow Kirby or Gerry to score. His play inspired me to elevate my own game and together we all but shut down the offence of each team. I had completely forgotten that Kirby was out to get me.

Then it happened. Pat Walsh brought the ball into the zone. He passed it off to Selby, who went by Gerry Walsh and dished it to Jim Stockdale, positioned to the left of the net. If he'd shot it right away, he probably would have scored; Finnie, for once, was out of position and would never have gotten there in time. But instead of shooting, Stockdale, true to form, opted to pass. Somehow I got my stick out and intercepted it. I turned and looked for someone on the other team and saw Jordi Svenson. I fired the ball onto his stick and was moving back into position when I heard, behind me, Kirby Walsh's fearsome words: "Watch out for Ahab!"

His stick shot into my groin. All I remember after that is pain; it's possible that I blacked out. When I came to, I was curled up in the foetal position on the pavement. Gradually, I became aware of a scuffle going on around me. I looked up and saw Kirby and Finnie locked in combat. Kirby had a hold of Finnie's jersey, but he couldn't land a punch on Finnie, who was in prime form, dodging and striking like a mongoose. Whenever Kirby swung, Finnie would step or duck out of his way and reply with a shot to Kirby's midsection. After evading one particularly brutal punch, Finnie tagged Kirby square in the kidney. Kirby went down, clutching his side. Finnie began to kick him, raining blows upon Kirby's head. Kirby attempted to protect his face, but his efforts were futile.

"Watch out for Ahab yourself, you stupid fuck," Finnie screamed, drawing forth a spurt of blood from his brother's nose. "The king is dead! Long live King Finnie! Long live King Paul!"

Patrick and Gerry pulled Finnie back, but they merely restrained him. They did not retaliate in any way; they would, in the future, go so far as to prevent Kirby from exacting revenge. I don't think they picked on Finnie as much after that and I never heard the oath again.

I saw that a person had to stand up for himself if he wanted to get anywhere, especially in hockey. From then on, I didn't hesitate to knock people down if they came in on me, even if they were bigger than I was. So what if I was scared of them? If I let them walk all over me, I'd have to be even more scared of them. Thinking back on the incident, I realize that the important lesson, the one that I didn't learn until it was much too late, was that if you're going to swim around in strange waters acting like a big fish, you'd better watch out for Ahab.

From then on, Finnie and I were afforded a lot more respect, even though most of the players were five or six years older than us. We were invited to play more often, but this was short-lived, because by the middle of September the real hockey season was about to begin. Portsmouth's Memorial Arena was home to a variety of junior teams and both Finnie and I were eligible to play. I had never played on ice before; I had never even been on skates. Finnie had skated numerous times and had his own pair, but he had never played goal on ice. We decided that we would have to make the transition.

I waited for weeks until I thought that my parents were in the right mood to ask for their permission and, more importantly, for enough money to buy equipment. The main difference between street hockey and ice hockey, besides the ice, is the amount of equipment involved. To play on the street you only need a stick, but to play in an ice hockey league you need shin, shoulder and elbow pads, pants, gloves, skates, a helmet, an athletic cup, a jersey and socks and a large bag in which to put it all. Since my father lost his arm our family had been on a tight budget; money was scarce, even with my mother's job and my father's pension. I knew that if I wanted to play, my timing would have to be perfect.

Finnie was relentless. Every day he'd ask for an update.

"Did you ask them yet?"

"No."

"Why?"

"Wrong time."

"If you don't ask soon, it will be too late."

It was never the right time. It wasn't so much that my parents were in bad moods; my mother was almost always the same stern but understanding woman I had known all my life, but my father was changing at such a pace that I really didn't know what to expect from him anymore.

♦

It had taken my father six days to save us from the garage. On the seventh he should have rested, but he didn't. It would have been nice if it was a Sunday, but it wasn't. It was a Tuesday. That day my father had gone downtown and gotten himself a library card. He had signed out the maximum number of books and had spent his days since on the back porch reading. For a while, he read a lot of Hemingway. He liked *A Farewell to Arms* best. He would read and reread the ending: the guy's girlfriend dies giving birth to their baby, who also dies while the guy's eating a sandwich in the hotel. When the guy finds out, he just turns around and walks away as if nothing ever happened, except you know that's not how he feels. My father admired this; for him, it was impossible to be detached from even the most trivial of life's details. My father cared how many birds were using our bird feeder. He cared how many spoons were in the cutlery drawer. He cared whether the towels in the linen closet were correctly folded and ordered.

He also read some Melville. Unlike Kirby Walsh, he actually finished *Moby Dick*. Whenever he was in a certain mood, he would point at whomever he wanted to chastise with the stump of his arm and growl, "Bad, bad work, Mr. Starbuck." None of us ever knew what it meant exactly and even after I read *Moby Dick* and found the part where Stubb says that, I still don't know what the heck my father was on about. As far as *Moby Dick* and my father are concerned, I can't really say which perplexes me more; I understand very little about either of them.

The real clincher, however, was when my father discovered that the library had every issue of *National Geographic* published since the society's inception in 1888. He began to start all his sentences with, "Did you know...." Invariably the sentence would end with an obscure fact somewhere between very and not at all interesting. "Did you know that Alexander Graham Bell was the first president of the society?" "Did you know that a blue whale is over 100 feet long, but can't swallow anything larger than a

herring?" "Did you know that there actually is a Blarney stone?"
Whether or not you knew, and whether or not you even answered,
his response was always the same: "How about that! Who would
have guessed?"

He started with the first issues and worked forward; he even
made a long-term plan. He was, he figured, some 93 years behind
or, if you prefer, 1,055 issues. Thankfully for him, the magazine
didn't become a monthly until 1898, or he would have been lost.
He decided that he would read three a week, from front to back.
At that pace it would take him five years to read them all, at which
time he would be five years, or 60 issues, behind on the newly
published magazines.

At first it took him a long time to read even one. He was not
well-practised and often stumbled over words. He also found it
difficult to turn the pages because of his arm, so he had to be extra
careful with the older, more fragile issues. Eventually, as the issues
got hardier and he became more proficient, he got to the point
where he could read an entire issue in about four hours, which,
given the amount of time he spent out on the back deck, was not
very long at all.

I did not know what to make of all this; being unable to gauge
my father's moods was unnerving. As Finnie constantly reminded
me, however, the deadline to register for hockey was fast
approaching. Whomever administered the children's leagues was
not very forgiving about late registration. Once the deadline
passed, you were out of luck.

Well aware of this, I decided to bite the bullet. I was, to say the
least, surprised by how the idea was received.

"You hear that, Mary? The boy wants to play hockey!"

The next words I expected to hear were, "Bad, bad work, Mr.
Starbuck," but I was wrong.

"You'll need all sorts of stuff," my mother said.

"I'll take you down to the store after school tomorrow, Paul."

"Really?" I couldn't believe it.

"Sure. Did you know that people used to think that if you ate gold you'd live longer?"

"Huh?"

"How about that! Who would have guessed?"

"I can really play?"

"Of course you can. It's what your real father would have wanted," my father laughed. I was born on the night Paul Henderson scored his winning goal. My father often joked that Henderson had more to do with my safe arrival then he did. I don't think my mother really understood what was supposed to be so funny about that. I think my father would actually have been honoured if Henderson *had* fathered me. He had, after all, scored the game-winning goal that restored Canada's national pride.

I don't think I slept much that night and the next day when I told Finnie he actually squealed he was so happy. "Can I come with you to the store?" he asked me.

"Sure," I said. His family owned the store; of course he could come.

We waited anxiously outside the school for my father to arrive. He wasn't allowed to drive because of his lost arm, but in Portsmouth you can walk pretty much everywhere. My father didn't go out often; he was still a little self-conscious about his arm, so when he did go out he walked. Unlike other adults I knew, he didn't walk so fast that it was hard to keep up with him. He wasn't in any hurry and he knew it. On this day, though, I thought he could have made an exception and I was mad as hell, waiting out front and picturing him sauntering along as if he hadn't a care in the world, while in fact he had a young son who was almost crippled by anticipation.

"There he is!" Finnie cried, frightening me, but it wasn't him. "Never mind. It's only Mr. Palagopolis."

Mr. Palagopolis was the school janitor and Portsmouth's only other one-armed man. He had lost his arm in the Korean War and he was truly one of the nicest men I knew. He was getting on in years, however, and had a tendency to remember things the way he *wished* they had happened and not the way they had actually occurred. The only time I had seen him get upset was when someone's dad called him Greek. "I don't know why you think I'm Greek," he had said, his face turning red. "I was wearing a Canadian uniform when they blew my arm off."

Actually, his arm had not been blown or even shot off. He had scratched it badly on some barbed wire he was laying out around his platoon's camp and, because he had mistrusted army doctors, he had left the scratch untreated and developed gangrene. He had nearly died and was lucky to survive with just the loss of his arm.

He usually wore a prosthetic limb to aid him in his janitorial work, but that day he was without it. As he approached us, he appeared flustered, his face red and his fist clenched. "Hello, Mr. Palagopolis," Finnie said.

"You boys seen my claw?" he asked.

"Huh?"

"Someone stole my claw."

"Your arm?"

"Yes, yes, my claw. Do you know where it is?"

"No," Finnie answered.

Mr. Palagopolis looked at me. I supposed, since my father was the only other person in town who would have a practical use for his claw, I was a likely suspect. "No, sir."

"I hope not. You boys are good boys and I like you, but that claw's dangerous."

"Dangerous?" Finnie's eyes widened. Finnie found danger very exciting.

"Oh, sure, it's dangerous all right. Got a mind all its own. And if it's not attached to me, I can't control it."

"What does it do?"

"Who knows? I never know what the claw's up to." Mr. Palagopolis walked away, shaking his head.

I shuddered. "I wonder who stole his arm?" I said.

"Who knows? Maybe someone else needed it more."

While we waited for my father to arrive, we both imagined what the claw could possibly be up to.

When I looked up and saw my father standing in front of us, I remembered where we were going and I put Mr. Palagopolis out of my mind. Finnie, however, was still captivated. "Someone stole Mr. Palagopolis' claw," he said to my father.

"He probably thinks I did it," he replied.

"He said it has a mind of its own."

"He ought to know, if it does."

By the time we arrived at the sporting goods store, my father and Finnie had discussed at length the possibility that Mr. Palagopolis' claw was on the loose roaming wild about town. As we walked through the doors, though, my father became all business. Finnie was equally enthusiastic, following my father from aisle to aisle, offering suggestions as he saw fit.

"What Paul is, really, is a defenceman," Finnie said, "so he ought to have good shin pads for blocking shots. Really good shin pads."

"Gloves," my father said. "Gloves are what make the difference."

"Gloves?" I said.

"If you can't feel your stick, how are you going to be able to handle the puck?"

"Of course, good skates are *critical*," Finnie added.

After much debate, we decided that shin pads, gloves and skates were the most important pieces of equipment and that pants, shoulder pads and elbow pads were less so. My mother had insisted that my father buy me a top-of-the-line helmet and I'm glad she had.

Eventually we had everything in hand and headed to the cash desk. I was worried about how much all of it would cost, but my father didn't seem to be bothered in the slightest. He was actually in quite a good mood, laughing and joking around. When we reached the counter, however, he stopped laughing and became very sombre.

Behind the counter, talking to the sales clerk, was Roger Walsh. When we were older, Finnie told me that his father spent as much of his time as he could at the sporting goods store, which was only one of his many businesses. Even though it was without a doubt his least profitable venture, he apparently enjoyed being among the balls and sticks and gloves and shoes and skates. They reminded him of what it must have been like to be young. He felt he had missed his own childhood as he'd been groomed from an early age to assume control of the family business. Sometimes, when it was sunny outside and he was stuck in some office trying to keep his house of cards from tumbling down around him, he tried to invent a childhood filled with outdoor activities and friends and afternoons of unadulterated fun, so that he would have something to look back on and smile about. Whenever he felt like that, he would go down to the sporting goods store, which he had purposely not put the Walsh name on, and pretend that he was reliving memories of good times gone by.

Although he actively encouraged his own children to enjoy *their* childhoods, it was at the expense of the future of the family business. None of his older children was equipped to take control of the Walsh empire. Occcassionally, he thought Finnie might turn out to be capable, but most of the time he didn't seem so sure. These considerations weighed heavily on Roger Walsh.

I like to think that on the afternoon we were there Roger Walsh was fondly remembering a soccer game in which he had never played. When he saw his youngest son approach the counter, he might even have momentarily considered passing him the ball, as Finnie was in a good scoring position. Then he realized where he was and snapped to attention, which left him a bit disoriented.

"Hi, Dad," Finnie said.

"Hello, Finnie," Roger Walsh answered.

"How are you, Mr. Walsh?" I asked.

"Oh, hello Paul. I'm fine. Hello, Bob. How are things with you?"

"They're all right, I suppose."

"That's great. Glad to hear it. Your arm is healing well?"

"It hasn't grown back, but other than that, yes."

Roger Walsh smiled hesitantly. Finnie laughed and I assumed that this meant my father had been joking, so I laughed too. Mr. Walsh emitted a small chuckle and my father smiled. Then there was an uncomfortable silence.

"We'd like to purchase this hockey gear for Paul, Mr. Walsh."

"Oh, sure. I'll get Kevin to ring it in. Nice talking to you." He motioned to Kevin, a dopey-looking man in his late twenties, who was one of the store's three full-time employees. As Mr. Walsh was leaving the store, he turned back and called over to jittery Kevin, "Give them the staff discount." A bewildered Kevin nodded; it was not common for Roger Walsh to give anyone a discount. The door jingled shut and Roger Walsh was gone.

"How much is the staff discount?" my father inquired.

"Fifty percent, sir," Kevin answered.

"Fifty percent?"

"Yes, sir."

"Holy...," my father looked over at Finnie, "cow."

We paid for the equipment and I was set. I can recall few times in my life when I have been happier than I was on that day.

Unlike Finnie, I did not use my equipment for street hockey. Concrete and pavement had taken their toll on Finnie's pads; they hadn't been in great shape to begin with and Finnie was having to patch up holes in the leather more and more frequently as time went on. I put my gear in my closet, only taking it out to look at it and try it on, which I did nearly every day.

I began to attend the public skate down at the arena with Finnie. I found skating forward awkward, but I could skate backward without nearly as much effort. The only way I could stop was to either fall down or slam into the boards.

Finnie was a terrific skater, but a lousy skating teacher. "Move your feet," he'd yell. "No, no, not like that!"

I would usually answer him by falling on either my face, my ass, or both.

"You're not trying," he'd say, standing over me. "You can do it, I know you can. Here, watch me."

So I'd watch him skate around and then I'd get up and the cycle would repeat itself.

One day, I fell down and, instead of seeing Finnie standing over me shaking his head, I saw Joyce, laughing. I felt my face flush. I quickly realized that it wasn't a malicious laugh, but rather a sympathetic laugh, if such a thing is possible. I got up slowly and tried to talk to her without falling down. I failed.

"Jesus, Paul, you're a crappy skater," she said, looking down at me.

"I know."

"He's just learning," Finnie said defensively.

"I can see that. He doesn't seem to be learning very much."

"Skating's hard," I said.

"Not really. Show me what you can do."

I got to my feet and pushed off with a couple of hesitant strides.

"Straighten your ankles," Joyce said.

I straightened my ankles and took a couple more strides.

"Bend your knees."

I bent my knees.

"Push with one foot and glide with the other."

I did as instructed.

"Transfer your weight as you push off."

With straight ankles and bent knees, I pushed, glided and transferred my weight. I wasn't trying to skate so much as I was trying not to look like an idiot in front of Joyce. She skated backward ahead of me, shouting tips and encouragement. Finnie did laps around the rink, switching from forward to backward effortlessly.

Then I realized that I was skating. "Hey, look at this," I shouted to anyone who would listen.

"See? I told you it wasn't so hard," Joyce said.

"Holy shit," Finnie said.

I picked up my pace, gaining speed with every stride. Then I remembered that I didn't know how to stop. I went hard into the boards and fell to the ice. Finnie and Joyce stood over me, looking concerned.

"You okay?" Finnie asked.

"I think so."

"We're going to have to teach you how to stop," Joyce said.

"That's probably a good idea," I said, pleased on several levels with the idea of further skating lessons with Joyce.

"Come back after school tomorrow. We'll see what we can do."

Over the next few weeks, I spent all my free time at the arena. As I walked home after that first lesson, though, I was overwhelmed by how much I had achieved. I was exhausted, but it was a good kind of tired. It would have been nice if I could have held onto that feeling, but it didn't last.

That night I had the dream for the first time. I would have the dream fairly regularly over the next 15 years. I didn't figure out what it meant until it was too late. That night, I dreamt only part of it; the rest would come later.

♦

I was in an arena, not the Portsmouth arena, but a much larger one. I was wearing full hockey equipment and I was skating fast into the opposition zone. I felt something heavy attach itself to the back of my jersey, but I couldn't see what it was. In my head I heard someone yell and then the puck went into the net and the crowd went insane with frenzied cheering. Everyone rushed over to me like I was a hero and then I heard my father say, clearly above the roar of the crowd, "Bad, bad work, Mr. Starbuck." I felt an overwhelming sense of dread and then I woke up.

♦

By the time my first practice rolled around, I was a fairly competent skater. Considering that I had been out on the ice for less than a month, I thought I could handle myself with a certain amount of confidence.

Because of our age and level of experience, Finnie and I had been posted to the same team: The Jaguars. We would play against three other teams: The Falcons, The Lions and The Mustangs. All the younger children's teams were named after animals, even though none of these beasts could be found anywhere near Portsmouth. They were exotic animals and hockey on ice was an exotic notion. Going from the street to a rink was, for us, like going from the minor leagues to the NHL. I had just turned nine and was ready to get on with my life. When Finnie and I talked of

Wayne Gretzky and Peter Stastny, we spoke as though we were all of the same calibre. We often speculated about what it would be like to play against them.

"To stop Peter Stastny, you have to watch his hands, not the puck," Finnie said.

"You have to keep Gretzky from skating into open ice," I said.

We reminisced about our old street games like a couple of pros remembering their junior careers. We laughed at our low level of skill, the bizarre things we had thought would work and what happened when they hadn't. Those days before the season started, we were high on the prospect of hitting the ice.

The night before our first practice, I was so giddy I could hardly eat my supper, but I noticed that my mother appeared to be worried about something. I imagined that she was concerned about how I would deal with my upcoming superstardom; I was wrong. After she cleared the dishes, my father told Louise and me to stay at the table. The possibility of some special dessert crossed my mind. When my mother returned from the kitchen empty-handed, however, I began to think that something was up.

"Your mother and I have something to tell you, kids," my father said solemnly.

I felt the blood drain from my face. They're getting a divorce, I thought. Several kids at school had parents who were divorced, but I couldn't imagine such a thing happening to *my* parents. It just wasn't possible.

Louise started to cry; apparently she'd thought of the same thing.

"What in God's name are you crying about, Louise?" my mother asked.

"I don't want Daddy to move away."

"What?"

"No one's going anywhere, Louise. In fact, there's going to be one more person living here," my father smiled.

I thought at first that maybe Grandma Woodward was moving in. Louise, to her credit, understood immediately. I've never seen someone stop crying so abruptly. "You're having a baby?" she asked my mother.

"That's right. You'll have a new brother or sister."

"Or maybe both," Louise said.

"What?" my father said, startled.

"Twins," she explained. "It could be twins."

"Holy shit!"

"It's not twins, Bob," my mother said.

"Are you sure? We can't afford twins."

"I'm sure it's not twins."

My father shifted in his seat, visibly relieved. "The thing is, babies cost a lot of money," he said, looking at me.

"A lot of money," my mother agreed.

"We're going to have to cut back."

"All of us will have to make sacrifices."

"It won't be easy."

Slowly I began to clue in. I realized that I would not be playing hockey and furthermore I would have to *volunteer* not to, for the good of the family.

Louise got the ball rolling. "I've got a ton of stuff in the basement I could sell," she said.

"Your toys?" I asked her.

"They're not toys," she said, "and I'm getting rid of them."

"Holy shit," I said.

"Language, Paul," my father said.

"He gets that from you, Bob."

"I know. What do you want me to do about it?"

"You could stop swearing in front of the children."

"It's nothing they won't hear eventually."

"I see no reason to speed things up."

"Jesus Christ, Mary, all right. I'll try to watch my mouth."

"Bob!"

This was a familiar routine. I don't think my mother actually cared whether Louise and I swore a blue streak and I know that my father didn't; the only person he wouldn't swear in front of was Finnie. On some level he still considered Finnie his boss' son. My mother made a fuss about us cursing because she thought that, as a mother, she ought to. Deep down, though, I don't think she really cared, because no matter how much we swore, as long as she didn't find our subject matter offensive, we faced no real repercussions.

"I'm proud of you, Wheeze," my father said.

Louise scrunched up her face. She was too old to be called Wheeze.

"You're a good girl. Your father and I appreciate what you're doing. Every little bit helps."

All eyes turned to me. I knew what they wanted, but I really, really didn't want to do it. It just wasn't fair. I had so much riding on this. "I'll get a paper route," I said.

"Oh no you won't," my father said.

It was a long-standing debate. My father had had a paper route when he was my age and had been "screwed royally" by both the newspaper company and his customers. He steadfastly refused to let me have anything to do with newspaper delivery.

"Maybe that's not such a bad idea, Bob," my mother said.

"No way in hell. No son of mine is going to slave for those bastards."

"Please, Dad?"

"Sorry, Paul. I just won't allow it."

This left me with one option only. I swear, to this day I can still remember how it felt: like I was being kicked in the back with a big spiky boot. "I guess I could quit hockey," I said, wondering how I could quit something I hadn't even started.

"It really does cost a lot of money, dear," my mother said.

"Even with the discount Mr. Walsh gave us?"

"Yes," my father said. "It's mainly the league fees."

"Maybe you can play next year."

"If we can afford it." My father patted me on the shoulder. "I'm sorry, son. I know how much you wanted to play."

♦

As I adjusted to the finality of the situation, I felt a little better. It was only a game, after all. Later that night, realizing that I wouldn't be attending my first practice the next morning, I began to wonder how I was going to tell Finnie. He seemed to have more riding on the upcoming season than I did. If it hadn't been for him, I probably wouldn't have cared so much in the first place. Of course, he would wonder why I wasn't at practice and he would almost certainly rush straight over to my house when it was finished.

I had trouble getting to sleep that night; consequently, I slept in the next morning. It was a Saturday, so my mother didn't rouse me until 11 a.m.

Finnie poked his head out from behind her. "You slept in? How could you sleep in? We had a practice today!"

"I know."

My mother silently left the room. She was, if anything, a very tactful woman.

"Well, why weren't you there?"

"I can't play."

"What? Why not?"

"My mother's pregnant. We don't have the money."

"Oh." Finnie stood there thinking. Not having money wasn't a problem he typically encountered.

"My parents said that maybe I can play next year."

"Next year?"

"Yes."

"But not this year?"

"No."

"Not at all?"

"No, not at all."

"What about your equipment?"

"I guess I'll have to return it."

Finnie was silent for a moment; he was thinking very hard. "Don't worry about anything. I think I have an idea." He turned around and left.

A few minutes later, my mother came in. "Why was Finnie wearing goalie pads?" she asked me.

"He was?" I was so used to seeing him in them that I didn't even notice anymore. Finnie lived in his pads; I suppose it was sort of weird, but I didn't think so at the time.

"Yes, he was. Didn't you see him?"

"He always wears them."

"Why?"

"I don't know. He says it'll toughen him up."

"Jesus," she said.

"Language, Mom."

"Don't be cheeky, Paul."

"I'm sorry."

"It's all right."

♦

Later that week, I went to the sporting goods store to return my equipment, minus the skates, which could not be returned because I had used them. I was relieved to see that Mr. Walsh wasn't there. I placed my gear on the front counter. Kevin, the dopey sales clerk, was standing there, staring off into space.

"Hello," I said.

"Good afternoon. What can I do for you?"

"I have to return this stuff."

"Right. Just let me…." He stopped speaking and looked at me with a new-found interest. "Wait, aren't you the Woodward boy?"

"Yes," I said slowly, wondering why he knew who I was.

"I was told to give you a full refund," Kevin said, digging into the register and handing me a wad of cash.

"Thank you," I said and walked toward the door.

"Wait," Kevin called. "I don't want this stuff." He gestured toward my equipment.

"Why not?"

"It's defective. I've been told to ask you to dispose of it." He handed me the gear.

"Really?"

"Really."

I took the bag and left the store, heading for Finnie's house. I knew that Finnie had been behind this and that he had probably enlisted the help of his father. I also knew that if *my* father found out about it I would be in a whole mess of trouble. "Woodwards," he had often said, "do not accept charity. They work for what they get."

When I got to Finnie's house, I went to the front door and rang the bell. Clarice, the housekeeper, answered and led me through the house to Finnie's room. She knocked on his door.

"Come in."

Clarice turned and walked away.

I had only been in Finnie's house once before and then only in the kitchen. This house was the biggest and most ornate I had ever seen, even on TV. Finnie's room, though, was the exception to the rest of the house. There was an antique brass bed, a desk, a chest of drawers and a poster of Peter Stastny on the wall. Finnie's goalie pads were neatly stacked in the corner. Other than that, the room was bare.

Finnie, sitting at the desk organizing a pile of hockey cards, was surprised to see me.

"Paul! What are you doing here?"

"I went to return my equipment today."

"Oh?"

"Kevin gave me my money back and told me I could keep the stuff."

"Kevin's a nice guy."

"I know you did this, Finnie."

"Well, you're welcome."

"My father's going to kill me."

"Why? He gets his money back."

"He won't take it."

"So you still won't be able to play hockey?"

"No, I don't think so."

Finnie was silent. "I'm sorry, Paul."

"It's okay. You were trying to help."

"What are you going to do?"

"I don't know. I can't let my father find out I still have this stuff."

"I could look after it for you."

This was an appealing idea. Even though I was mad at Finnie, I was also very grateful. I knew why he had done it and I sure wanted to keep that equipment. "What would your father say?" I asked him.

"He'll never know. He's probably already forgotten about the whole thing."

"Maybe I could use the stuff next year."

"Sure."

So it was decided. I gave my father back the money he had

spent and kept my gear at Finnie's, with no one the wiser. Not that anyone around our house would have noticed. My parents were totally preoccupied with the prospect of a baby. Excited as my father was though, he was determined not to fall behind on his *National Geographic* reading. He read for at least an hour and a half each morning out on the back deck, even though it was the middle of October and it wouldn't be long before there was snow on the ground.

"Did you know," he would say, "that dolphins use sonar to locate their food?"

"No, Bob, I didn't," my mother would say, not really listening.

"How about that! Who would have guessed?"

The most marked change occurred in Louise. Without her kingdom to rule, she was like a deposed queen. She spent her days sitting sullenly in front of the television and, when one of my parents finally made her go outside, she would sit even more sullenly on the front stairs and watch the other children zip around the neighbourhood. She didn't indicate that she wanted to join them. I suspect that she did, but was unsure how to go about it. It wasn't just that she was unusually shy, although she was by no means outgoing. She was also a fairly attractive girl, as far as I could tell, but I'll admit that it's difficult to gauge that sort of thing with respect to your sister. She was tall, not quite lanky and had a face that made you want to trust her right away, but she had a way of hiding it behind a shroud of sandy-coloured hair.

Her main problem was that she just didn't have much she wanted to say. As a rule, if Louise didn't think something was terribly important, she didn't see the point in saying anything at all. For her, small talk was non-existent. Because small talk is a necessary step in forming friendships, even among children, Louise was, as a consequence of her verbal minimalism, at a distinct disadvantage.

The fact that there was something wrong with Louise certainly didn't escape my parents' attention. I suspect that, as concerned as they were, they just didn't have the time to figure out exactly what it was. Gaining access to her thoughts was slightly harder than interpreting the information contained on a computer disk without benefit of a computer.

My mother probably would have told Louise to be positive, to find a way to make things better. My father probably would have given her a rock. It's also possible that my parents actively chose to ignore the problem. Louise was, after all, an 11-year-old girl and they are well known for acting strangely.

To me, girls made no sense. They were mysterious creatures and Louise wasn't any different. I was worried about her, though, and I tried not to irritate or disturb her when she was by herself. She had always been very protective about the time she spent in the basement and I assumed that meant she enjoyed being alone. I knew that most people, from time to time, needed a little time to themselves and I figured that Louise just needed more than others.

Finnie made me see that I was wrong. Whenever he came over to our house, which was fairly often, he would make a point of talking to Louise. I had never noticed how much she actually had to say when talking to Finnie. Whenever they were together, she came out of her shell, which for Louise was no small feat. Finnie had this effect on almost everyone. Without even trying, he could make people do things they wouldn't ordinarily do.

When I finally asked him what he thought was wrong with Louise, he looked at me like I was an alien, a very stupid alien.

"What?" I asked.

"You don't know?"

"No, no one does. Not even my dad."

"But it's so obvious, Paul. She's *lonely*."

Finnie was right. It was obvious, and she was lonely.

"What should we do?"

"I don't know. She'll snap out of it, sooner or later."

Reassured that I was in no way abdicating my brotherly responsibilities, I let the situation work itself out. Louise's ability to cope with things in her own way was far greater than my own.

♦

Finnie invited me to his first hockey game. I didn't really want to go for fear that I would see what I was missing. The game was on a Saturday afternoon and there was a surprising number of people in attendance. I was about to sit down by myself when I saw Mr. Walsh waving me over to where he was sitting with Patrick, Gerry and Kirby.

"Hello there, Paul," Mr. Walsh said, smiling.

"Hello, Mr. Walsh," I answered.

"I was sorry to hear you wouldn't be playing hockey this season."

I could tell he was sincere. "Maybe I'll be able to play next year," I said.

"That's the right attitude. Things will work themselves out."

"I hope so."

Mr. Walsh nodded. He was the sort of man who was accustomed to things working out. "Big game today."

"Yes, sir."

"Finnie's first start."

"Sure is."

"How do you think he'll do?"

"Well…," I paused, wondering if Mr. Walsh wanted to hear what I really thought. I decided to hedge my bet. "I think he'll do ok as long as he keeps sharp with his glove."

"Hmm. Well, I guess we'll find out soon enough."

Thirty seconds into the game, Finnie let one in from outside the blue line. It was a high, rising shot that slipped over his glove into the net. Half of the people cheered, celebrating the goal, and the other half hung their heads in shame, feeling sorry for Finnie.

Fortunately, his team responded several minutes later, scoring on a play that was, given the ages of the players, an admirable combination of passing and skating. With the score tied, his team was back in the game and Finnie wasn't about to make any more mistakes. For the rest of the period, he played brilliantly, stopping several shots that by all rights should have scored.

Every time Finnie made a good save, his father jumped to his feet. "That's the way to do it, Finnie boy. That's the way to do it!"

Even Finnie's brothers seemed appreciative. Pat leapt out of his seat when Finnie managed to stop the puck from going in on a three-on-one rush that had given up several rebounds before Finnie smothered the play. As the game went on, his brothers tried less and less to hide the fact that they were enjoying themselves.

I was having mixed feelings about the game. I was completely impressed with Finnie's performance; it was clear that he was a much better goaltender than I had thought and I was happy that he was finally the centre of attention, but I wasn't impressed with the defencemen. Finnie was having to make saves he shouldn't have had to make; I should have been there. On top of all that, I was bitten by the magic, that almost supernatural feeling that comes with being in the stands watching a game when you know you could be playing. It does strange things to your mind.

Finnie's team won by a score of 6-1, a resounding victory. After the game, Finnie was showered with praise from his teammates and their parents as well as from his own family. He didn't seem to be affected by it; his face was blank and he was little more than polite to his admirers. When I asked him what was wrong, he hesitated before answering quietly, "I shouldn't have let in that first goal and you should have been out there."

I didn't know what to say. He was right, he shouldn't have let in that first goal, but everyone, including me, thought that he'd more than made up for it by the way he'd played for the rest of the game. On the subject of whether or not I belonged on the ice, I was in complete agreement, but I didn't want to belabour the point. "Next year," I said. "Maybe I can play next year."

"Next year isn't good enough," he said.

"There's nothing we can do about it."

Finnie smiled. "Maybe. Maybe not."

♦

When my mother became pregnant, for the third time, she was 41. That is not necessarily too old for a woman to have children, but in my mother's case it was pushing the limits. By the time December rolled around, she was five months pregnant and she was having a difficult time coping. My father talked to Louise and me about this and we were instructed to give my mother a fair degree of latitude. Because of this, I was slower to suspect that something was wrong when I arrived home from school and discovered her seated on the kitchen counter, engaged in a heated debate with the blender.

"You think you know a lot about blending, with your fancy settings and whirring blades? Well, let me tell you, you don't know nothing about it. Nothing!" she slurred.

I remembered my father's warnings and silently went to the refrigerator and poured myself a glass of juice.

"You drinking juice, Paul? I hope you're not drinking that juice. That juice is for special occasions."

"Oh. Sorry," I said.

"I'm just pulling your leg, Paul-o. That's just ordinary juice there. No such thing as special juice, Paul-o. No such thing." My mother collapsed to the floor, laughing. "No such thing!"

I decided that this behaviour was more than likely outside the bounds of what my father had told me to expect, so I went out to the backyard to get him. I told him what was going on and he immediately rushed inside, arriving just in time to see my mother trying to beat the toaster to death.

"You'll be toast, toaster," she screamed, slamming it against the counter.

"What the hell are you doing, Mary?" my father yelled, grabbing at her with his missing arm.

"Something I should've done a long time ago," she answered, resuming her assault. "I'm showing this damned toaster who's the boss around here." She threw the toaster onto the floor, where it shattered, sending pieces flying across the kitchen. "Who's laughing now, huh?" my mother said as she fell to the floor, unconscious. We picked her up, piled into the car and drove to the hospital.

I was sure my mother was going to die and that Louise and I were going to be put into a foster home, since it was obvious to all of us that my father was not fit to raise two children on his own. I was understandably relieved when the doctor came out and told us that she was recovering. She had, it turned out, developed gestational diabetes. Her erratic behaviour was the result of her blood sugar being off-kilter. With insulin and closer medical supervision, she would be fine. The health of the baby was less certain, but all we could do was wait and see.

As if that weren't trouble enough, Finnie began avoiding me. Whenever I asked him if he wanted to do something after school, he would get a peculiar look on his face and tell me he was busy.

He was like that for most of the month of December and over the Christmas holidays I didn't see him at all. I phoned his house several times, but Clarice informed me that young master Walsh was out and wasn't expected back until much later.

I didn't have a clue why Finnie would want to avoid me. He was the most loyal person I had ever known; I would have had to do something very, very bad to lose his friendship.

Without Finnie, I began to experience the same sense of isolation that plagued Louise. Unlike her, though, I was unprepared to sit quietly by myself, so I resorted to following my father around. I didn't think he had noticed Finnie's absence, but he had.

"Where's Finnie these days?" he asked.

"I don't know," I said. "I don't think he wants to be friends with me anymore."

"I wouldn't worry too much," my father said. "I have a feeling that boy's up to something." He reached into his pocket and handed me another rock. I spent the better part of the day trying to figure out what the rocks were for and couldn't, but it did help me to forget about Finnie.

◆

I was allowed to stay up until midnight on New Year's Eve as we said goodbye to 1981 and welcomed in 1982. Because my mother was pregnant and my father was not comfortable in social situations on account of his arm, the whole family was together for the end of the year. In past years Louise and I had been left at home with a babysitter while my parents had attended one of many neighbourhood parties.

That night as my father and I sat on the front steps, tightly bundled against the cold, we could hear laughter drift in from nearby cocktail parties. My father insisted upon being the first person to enter the house in the new year, so we were outside waiting for midnight. He had a glass of Jamieson's whiskey and I had a glass of milk that he had secretly augmented with a tiny, but palatably present, amount of Irish cream. My mother and Louise had decided to stay inside because it was deadly cold outside. We could see them through the window playing cards in the front room. My mother had a glass of orange juice and Louise had milk, which I doubted had been supplemented in any way.

We had just raised our glasses while my father was searching for something toast-worthy to say, when a snowball hit him squarely in the head. Miraculously, he managed to avoid spilling his whiskey as he dove for cover. A veteran of many snowball fights myself, I likewise sought protection, my eyes searching the dimly lit street for our attacker.

Although his aim was good, Mr. Palagopolis was not one for stealth. He stood on the sidewalk, shaking his fist and screaming. "Too far, Bob Woodward! You've gone too far!" He was once again missing his claw and was having considerable difficulty constructing another snowball to hurl at us.

"What's wrong, Mr. Palagopolis?" my father shouted, keeping his head down.

"You know damn well what's wrong. You got my claw again. Third one since September."

"What's he talking about?" my father asked as a snowball whizzed by his head. For a one-armed man, Mr. Palagopolis had fantastic aim.

"I think someone's stolen his arm again."

"I didn't take your arm, Mr. Palagopolis."

"Sure, that's what you want me thinking. I know you're the only other one who needs it. Got to be you."

"But we're missing opposite arms."

Mr. Palagopolis had his arm cocked, ready to throw another

snowball. He paused for a moment, thinking, then lowered his arm. "We are?"

"Sure. Look, I've got my right arm and you've got your left. It wouldn't even fit me."

Mr. Palagopolis dropped the snowball and ran up the driveway to the steps. My father cringed, expecting to be hit again at close range. Instead, Mr. Palagopolis looked at his missing arm, confirmed what my father had told him, then slumped down on the steps. "I'm so sorry, Bob Woodward. It's just that every time I get a new arm somebody takes it from me. It's getting me mad."

My father stood up and brushed himself off. The front door opened cautiously as Louise and my mother poked their heads out.

"Mary, would you please get Mr. Palagopolis here a glass of what I'm having?" my father asked. My mother nodded and disappeared into the house.

"It's just that a man should have two arms, or at least one arm and one claw, and for some reason I can't seem to manage either."

"It's not right, Mr. Palagopolis. We should both have two arms."

"You can call me Pal, Bob Woodward. People call me Pal."

"Sure, Pal. You can call me Bob."

"I do, Bob Woodward."

My mother returned with a glass of whiskey for Mr. Palagopolis. He took a big gulp and sighed. "I miss my arm, Bob Woodward. Been 30 years and I still miss her."

"I miss my arm too."

"Between the two of us, we have enough arms for one whole man."

"You know, Pal, you're right. That counts for something."

"Bad thing we can't loan them off."

My father leaned his head to one side and a small smile upturned his lips. "Sure we can."

"We can?"

"Sure. Stand up."

Mr. Palagopolis stood up. My father stood behind him. He placed his arm where Mr. Palagopolis' arm should have been, moving it as he thought appropriate.

"Jesus!"

"Sure! Just pretend that it's your arm; have a good time. For the next little while, it *is* your arm."

Mr. Palagopolis shifted his drink from his left hand to his right and took a sip. He adjusted his hat, reached into his pocket and removed a cigarette. He lit it and puffed contentedly, tapping the ash with the tip of his right index finger. As he took another sip of his whiskey, several tears ran into his bristly moustache. "Thank you, Bob Woodward. Let me be your arm now."

I don't know how long this went on. Because of the late hour and because of the liquor in my milk, I fell asleep right there on our front steps in the middle of winter, snug under the protection of two one-armed men. I suppose someone eventually took me inside, because the next thing I remember is waking up with a sore throat and a runny nose.

Whenever I was sick, I spent my time with Louise. If you needed to rest calmly but didn't want to be bored, Louise was your girl. That day, though, she was nowhere to be found. I asked my father where she was; he didn't know. I asked my mother and she told me that Louise had gone out early that morning with a friend.

Louise had never had a friend before. None of the girls in her class seemed to want to have much to do with her and Louise, generally speaking, didn't like boys. I was intrigued.

Over the next week, the last week of winter vacation, Louise continued her disappearing act. When she did return she was tight-lipped about where she'd been.

My father started to spend a lot of time with Mr. Palagopolis, or Pal, as he insisted we call him. Besides their missing arms, they had other things in common. Pal also enjoyed *National Geographics* and he was easily my father's equal when it came to eccentricity. Pal was in his late 50s though, and was prone to bronchitis, so they refrained from sitting on the back deck during the winter months. This was especially hard on my mother, who, while trying to rest, was repeatedly awakened by the two of them arguing about some minor point of starfish anatomy, the lactose content in cheese or whether volcanoes are more dangerous than earthquakes. My mother would ask them to keep their noise to a minimum and they would try their best, but sooner or later they would be yelling at the top of their lungs and my mother would have to ask them to settle down. Several times she even threatened to kick the two of them out of the house, but I don't think she really meant it.

It was good to see my father enjoying himself again. After what he'd done to the garage, we had begun to think he was going a bit nuts. I'm not sure why we thought that hanging around with Pal precluded that possibility, but we did, so we were all a little happier.

I found their conversations fascinating if somewhat perplexing. Although I would rather have been out playing hockey with Finnie, listening to my father and Pal argue was a welcome alternative.

♦

By mid-January of 1982, any remaining doubts regarding the greatness of Wayne Gretzky were cast aside. He had scored 50 goals in the first 39 games, shattering Maurice "the Rocket" Richard's record. Gretzky would go on to score 92 goals and 120 assists that season, setting a record that many think will never be broken. Peter Stastny had 139 points that year, his second in the league. Gretzky and Stastny were playing the best hockey of their careers, but both the Edmonton Oilers and the Quebec Nordiques were eventually eliminated in the playoffs.

I had been following the progress of both teams since the start of the season and in early January it still looked as though they would be contenders for the playoffs. Meanwhile, Finnie was still avoiding me.

Then, one afternoon in the second week of January, I was on the driveway practising my stickhandling when I turned around and saw Finnie.

"Come on," he said, "I have something important to show you."

He led me through the snow-covered streets toward the sawmill. I tried to get him to tell me what was up, but he wouldn't even give me a hint. When we got to the sawmill and turned up the path, I knew where we were going. I was so surprised to see Louise at the reservoir that I didn't notice what they had done. "What are *you* doing here?" I said testily.

She just smiled.

Then I saw it. The large cement slab was now coated by a sheet of ice. At the edges, boards stamped with the Walsh logo had been placed perpendicular to the ice. A net stood at either end. "Did you do this?" I asked Finnie.

"*I* helped him," Louise said.

Finnie shrugged. "You wanted to play on ice. Here's the ice."

Finnie had turned the pumping-station shack into a locker room. Before we could put on our equipment, we had to warm it over a large metal barrel filled with waste wood that Finnie had procured from the sawmill.

Because the water in the reservoir was insulated by earth and snow it didn't freeze all the way down. We used a hand pump in the shack and connected it to a hose. Finnie was a dedicated ice maker. He used a lawn sprinkler to ensure that the water was evenly distributed across the ice's surface. He moved the water around with a giant squeegee and then meticulously rolled up the hose and drained the pump. He often reminded me that it was very important no water be left in either the hose or the pump because if they froze they would be ruined. We could get a new hose if we had to, but there would be no replacing the pump.

Finnie also made periodic inspections of the boards and nets, making repairs when necessary. My only job was to operate the hand pump. It was a tough job physically, but Finnie assured me that it would toughen me up. I did what he told me to do.

Occasionally, kids Finnie and I knew and trusted were invited up to the rink to play. Mostly they were players from Finnie's team or friends from school. Once in a while we'd be joined by Jim Stockdale, Jordi Svenson or Bruce Selby. We hadn't actually invited them, but we didn't mind if they played. For the most part, we were left alone because of the remote location of the rink. We were never joined by any of Finnie's brothers, which was just as well. I was allowed to develop my skating and shooting skills without having to watch out for Ahab.

Finnie spent an enormous amount of time playing hockey that winter. The rink stayed frozen until the end of March, the same month his league play ended.

Second Period

In his first season, Finnie was easily his team's most valuable player, posting many performances similar to the one I had first witnessed. For my part, I was steadily improving because of the ice time I managed to get on the reservoir rink. By the time the ice melted, I was a capable and confident player, sure of my abilities and gaining both speed and strength.

Things were hectic at home. Our family was in the midst of a full-scale recession; every penny was pinched and scrimped and saved. My father even cut down on his goldfish supply. He didn't go cold turkey, but instead of buying 25 goldfish every month he bought only five. As it turned out, this was good for the goldfish too; because there were fewer of them, the oxygen supply lasted longer. However, because there were fewer dead goldfish as food for the survivors, my father was forced to start feeding them.

My mother didn't have any more "spells"; she was very good about controlling her diet and taking her insulin so she managed to keep the diabetes in check for the rest of her pregnancy. That's the way she was: steady, unflappable.

It was announced that Louise and I would have to share a bedroom to make room for the baby, a prospect that didn't really appeal to either of us. Although I think that we got along fairly well compared to other brothers and sisters our age, Louise was a private person and quite protective of her personal space. We both knew this and foresaw trouble.

Louise came up with a solution: she would move into the basement. At first my parents were against the plan, but they slowly came around. My father and Pal spent an afternoon building a makeshift room, a crude construction but, all things considered, a good little space. Louise wouldn't have cared if it was a cardboard box; she was just happy to have her own place. She moved in as soon as it was finished and her old room was just as quickly filled with cribs and stuffed animals and other baby-related things. It seemed strange to me that something so small could require so much stuff.

While I was a little hesitant about the whole ordeal, Finnie was beside himself with anticipation. "Do you think it will be a boy or a girl?" he asked me.

"I don't know."

"I hope it's a boy."

"Why?"

"Because then we can show him all the stuff we know, without him having to figure it out for himself."

"Oh."

"And there will be no oaths."

I saw where Finnie was coming from; he hated his brothers and was determined that this child would have the benefit of siblings less homicidal than his own. He liked my family precisely because, without trying, my parents had made Finnie feel like he was one of us.

"Of course, it's fine if it's a girl," Finnie said, "it'll just make things a little harder."

"Harder?"

"Well, sure. Girls are harder to understand."

"Even Louise?"

"Especially Louise."

He got no argument from me. When Louise had helped Finnie build the rink, I had wondered if it was a sign of things to come. But if Louise had spent a lot of time in the basement before the move, that amount now doubled. She was only seen at meals; from the time she got home from school to the time she went to bed, she was in her room, with the door shut.

I didn't really have much time to dwell on Louise's peculiarities, however, because in the middle of April my mother went into labour and gave birth to Sarah Esther Woodward, my younger sister. My mother was one of those rare women who actually give birth on their due dates; Sarah was born exactly on schedule.

It was the 5th of April, a calm, mild day. Finnie and I were having a heated argument on my front steps about whether or not the New York Islanders were going to win their third Stanley Cup in a row in the upcoming playoffs. We both hated the Islanders, but Finnie said that they were going to win for sure, which they eventually did. At the time, however, I was certain that they wouldn't.

"Come on, Finnie," I said, "Edmonton's a way better team."

"Maybe. Anything can happen in the playoffs, though."

Our discussion was interrupted by the sound of my mother screaming. We rushed inside and found her in the front hall, leaning heavily against the wall, in obvious pain. My father and Louise arrived seconds later, whereupon my mother announced that she had gone into labour.

"Are you sure?" my father asked.

My mother answered him with a look that could have stripped paint.

"Maybe we should go to the hospital," Louise said.

"Right. Of course," my father said.

I wondered if he'd been like this when Louise and I were born.

We all piled into the car, my father and Finnie and I in the front and my mother and Louise in the back. My father hadn't driven since his accident and with all the excitement he had apparently forgotten that he was the only one who could.

"Let's go, Robert," my mother said.

"I don't know," he said. "I don't think I can. Maybe we should call an ambulance."

"Are you fucking kidding me? We don't have time for that. Just drive the car, please, Bob." I rarely heard my mother use such strong language. Apparently, neither had my father. He turned the key, put the gearshift into reverse and backed out of the driveway.

By the end of the block, however, it was obvious that my father was having a difficult time steered the car and changing gears. There was sweat on his brow and his jaw was clenched. Then, while making a left-hand turn, he narrowly avoided hitting a bright green pickup. Shaken, he pulled the car over. "This isn't working," he said. "I'm going to get us all killed."

Finnie had an idea. "What if I steer?" he said.

My father considered the merits of the suggestion. "Have you ever driven a car before?"

"Oh, sure," he said. "My brother Pat lets me drive all the time."

I knew this was a lie; Pat wouldn't even let Finnie ride in the same car if he could help it.

"You're positive you can do this?"

"Definitely."

So, for the rest of the way, my father worked the pedals and the gearshift and Finnie sat sideways on his lap to steer. Finnie was not a small boy, so it was cramped for both of them, but we made it safe and sound. My mother was put into a wheelchair and she and my father were whisked toward the delivery room. Just before they went through the doors, my father turned around. "Good job, Finnie," he said. He looked at the three of us sternly. "There will be no more driving until you are 16. Understood?"

My mother was in labour for a little over an hour, far less time than it had taken her to have me or Louise. Once Sarah was out of the womb, however, things got complicated. She was born with what appeared to be jaundice, but tests soon revealed that this was not the case. After a wide array of treatments and procedures performed by various doctors, her skin remained yellow. There wasn't, as far as anyone could tell, anything physically wrong with her. She was just yellow. She was a strange baby who did not laugh or cry; she just lay there and *watched*. She was so quiet it was easy to forget she was even around.

I didn't know what to make of her at first. Both Finnie and I were disappointed; we had wanted a boy and we had ended up with a girl, a peculiar girl at that. But Finnie quickly got past this and it wasn't long before he began to think of Sarah as his own sister. I soon followed suit.

♦

That summer Mr. Walsh hired us to paint the wrought-iron fence that surrounded his estate. For three weeks we covered bar after bar after bar with black metallic paint. It was backbreaking work, but it allowed me to save enough money for the league registration fee. I even had a bit left over for some new skates; my old ones were too small.

After we finished the job, Finnie came over to my house almost every day. My mother was on maternity leave and I soon realized that Finnie was more interested in following her and Sarah around than playing with me. Once again I was left to my own devices.

With the warmth of summer, my father and Pal had taken to the back deck, Pal being safe from bronchitis. They continued their education with wholehearted enthusiasm, debating an infinitesimal number of points. On Thursdays they went to the library; this was a solemn but exciting occasion and children were not invited.

One particular Thursday Finnie was helping my mother with the laundry and I was bored to tears, so I crept down to the basement to see what Louise was doing. The room that my father and Pal had built was by no means impenetrable. There were cracks in the walls that eyes, if so inclined, could easily peer through. As silently as I could, I peeked into Louise's room.

She was sitting cross-legged in the centre of the floor, surrounded by toys I had assumed had been sold at a garage sale back in September. How she had managed to fool us I had no idea. I remembered what *I* had been forced to give up, though, and in a flurry of rage I burst into the room.

Before I could even start in on what would have undoubtedly been a heck of a rant, Louise grabbed me and pinned me to the floor, holding me tightly by the throat. "Listen to me, Paul. If you tell anyone about this, you will definitely regret it."

I was stunned. Never in my life had I seen such a ferocious look. I honestly thought she was going to hurt me. Her calm manner, her assured threat, was very convincing. "All right. Let me up," I said. Her grip on my neck was tight and I was having trouble breathing.

"Just remember, this is a secret. Don't tell anyone."

She let me up and I scrambled out of the room. As I climbed the stairs, I heard her door close softly.

In the laundry room, Finnie was helping my mother fold sheets. When my she saw me, she stopped folding. "Jesus, Paul, you look like you've seen a ghost."

"I'm fine," I said.

"Well, go and eat something. You're pale."

Finnie was watching me like a hawk, but he didn't say anything.

While I was sitting in the kitchen recovering from my ordeal with the help of a couple of cookies and a large glass of lemonade, Finnie came in and sat down next to me. He picked up a cookie and ate it before speaking. "You were spying on Louise?"

"Yes," I said, wondering how he knew that.

"So you saw the stuff."

"You knew about it?"

"Sort of. Well, I was pretty sure she'd kept some of it."

"How come you never told me?"

"I thought you'd be mad at her."

"I am. I had to give up hockey and she didn't have to give up anything."

"You didn't have to give up hockey. Why do you think she helped me build the rink?"

I was speechless. Later, I went down to the basement to apologize to Louise.

"Don't worry about it," she said.

"I really am sorry, Louise. And thanks."

She looked at me vacantly. "Thanks for what?"

"For building me the rink."

She laughed. "Oh, right. Sure. Well, you're welcome."

I left the room more puzzled than ever about what went on in Louise's head. I resolved to stick to things that I understood, hockey, for instance.

♦

That fall a young Swedish goaltender named Pelle Lindbergh entered the NHL. He was the first big-name European goaltender. In the 1982–83 season, his rookie season, he had three shutouts and let in an average of only 2.98 goals per game, making him the league's fourth-best goalie and earning him a spot on the all-star team at the age of 23. Finnie and I saw him play early in the season and, even though neither of us liked his team, the Philadelphia Flyers, we were taken aback by how good he was.

That year, when our hockey season started, we were permitted to choose our own numbers for our sweaters. Finnie chose 31, Lindbergh's number, and I chose 5, Bill Barilko's number.

Bashing Bill Barilko was born in Timmins, Ontario, in 1927. He entered the NHL as a defenceman with the Toronto Maple Leafs in the 1946–47 season and gained a reputation as a real grinder who made up for what he lacked in talent with enthusiastic physical play. In the 1951 Stanley Cup finals, in the fifth straight overtime game against the Montreal Canadiens, Bill Barilko fired a desperate shot from high in the slot and scored, winning the Leafs the cup. He had never scored more than seven goals in a single season and he certainly had never been considered for a spot on an all-star team. But that goal in overtime, one of only five he ever scored in the playoffs, was his last. Two months later Barilko was killed in a plane crash. The Leafs, who had won the Stanley Cup five of the previous seven years, wouldn't win it again until 1962, 11 years later.

Even though I had never seen Barilko play and didn't like the Leafs more than any other team, I had an unexplainable connection to Bashing Bill. I wore his number proudly and secretly; I told no one but Finnie of its significance.

◆

By the time I celebrated my 13th birthday in September 1985, it had become apparent to everybody but Finnie that Peter Stastny and Wayne Gretzky were not the same calibre of player. The season before, Gretzky had scored 208 points, 73 more than his closest competitor. Peter Stastny had scored only 100 points, half as many as Gretzky and not good enough for a top-10 finish.

Finnie remained undaunted; although Stastny was slipping, Finnie stuck by him.

Meanwhile, Lindbergh led the Philadelphia Flyers to the Stanley Cup finals and, even though they lost to Gretzky and the Edmonton Oilers in four straight games, Lindbergh earned his second spot on the all-star team and was awarded the Vezina Trophy for the most valuable goaltender. In Finnie's opinion it was in no way Lindbergh's fault that the Flyers were swept in the finals; it was the rest of the team who screwed up.

Only a few games into the new season, the Flyers were first in the league and it looked as though Lindbergh would have another banner year.

Things at home were shaping up too. My father was steadily progressing in his quest to read each issue of *National Geographic*; he had read 624 issues and was almost into the 1930s. Mr. Palagopolis had also taken up the challenge, but he was considerably slower than my father; he was just turning the century. My mother's diabetes had lessened to the extent that she no longer required insulin injections and she was back at work. Even Louise, now 15, showed signs of abdicating her throne. The phone often rang for her and she even ventured out occasionally on a Friday or Saturday night.

Sarah was three and a half years old and was still yellow. She had been a quiet baby, but as a small child it was all we could do to shut her up. My father and Pal loved it; the more questions she asked of them, the happier they were. She never got tired of their arguing; sometimes one simple question would send the two of them into a discussion that could last half an hour. Sarah just waited, listening to everything they said, and as soon as there was even a tiny lull in the conversation she would pose yet another question, which would lead to yet another discussion. It was as if she was trying to ask the perfect question, the one that would keep my father and Pal talking forever.

Sarah also talked to Finnie for hours on end. He was infinitely patient with her, but with him her task was harder. Finnie tried to give her the most concise answers possible, which meant that she had to have more questions on hand.

Sarah had learned that I rarely knew the answers to her questions. Instead she took it upon herself to share with me the extent of knowledge she had acquired each day, coming into my room before she went to bed to demonstrate what she had learned. On the day that Sarah discovered how to use the light switches, my mother had to take her to bed kicking and screaming. She came into my room and pushed a chair up to the wall, below the switch. Climbing onto the chair, she said to me, very seriously, "Watch." She flicked the light on and off, over and over again, clapping her hands with delight. To her it was magic. I suppose, for all I know, it might as well be. "I am the sun," she giggled. "Nighttime." Flick. "Daytime." Flick. "Nighttime."

Unlike Louise, Sarah was a very sociable child. But because of her yellowness, many children were initially reluctant to play with her. Some parents were even worried that she had a contagious disease. She usually won people over, though, in the end. Sarah was impossible to resist.

I had just started my fourth season of hockey in the city league. Every summer I earned money to pay for equipment and league fees by painting Mr. Walsh's fence. In hindsight it is possible that Roger Walsh paid me more money than was reasonable for the job and it is also possible that the fence didn't need to be painted each year. But I was grateful for the opportunity; without it, I wouldn't have been able to play hockey.

I had been steadily improving my game, though I was not a flashy player, or so said Finnie, and had only scored a handful of goals. I could pass the puck up the middle pretty well and opposing players had a hard time getting by me. Still, I had an awful lot to learn and it seemed that everyone else was getting better at a faster rate.

Finnie was becoming a star. He had recorded several shutouts the season before and had been voted our team's most valuable player. He was, simply put, one hell of a goaltender. He seemed to have conquered his weak glove side and his ability to read plays was fantastic. I had even heard "NHL" whispered occasionally in reference to Finnie.

On November 13, 1985, Finnie's 13th birthday, we were scheduled to play a game against the team that had beaten us in the league finals the year before. The rivalry was intense, not only between the players, but also between the parents. Both our families were in attendance and I was a lot more nervous than I usually was before a game. In the locker room, I sat quietly off in one corner, collecting my thoughts, waiting for the coach to give his usual pre-game speech.

Coach Hunter was a grizzled man who had reportedly played half a season for the Boston Bruins. Whether that was true or not he would never say for sure. "Doesn't matter what you've tried to do," he would say, "only matters what you've done." He now worked as a millwright in the Walsh sawmill. I'm not sure it was a job he actually enjoyed. He was an excellent coach, though.

As I laced up my skates, I realized that Finnie wasn't there yet, which was unusual. At least 45 minutes remained before the opening face-off, but Finnie was usually one of the first players to arrive. It took him a while to put on all his equipment and he liked to be alone before a game started. When it did, he was always the first member of the team to step onto the ice and the last one to step off it.

Fifteen minutes before the game, when Finnie still hadn't

shown up, Coach Hunter began to panic. "Woodward! Where's Walsh?" he asked me.

"I don't know, Coach," I said. I was just as worried as he was. Finnie had been looking forward to this game for weeks. It was his birthday; we were destined to win.

"Jesus Christ, where is that boy?" He looked at Tom Kazakoff, our backup goaltender. "I hope you sharpened your skates, Kazakoff."

Tom looked like he was going to throw up. He was a terrible goalie and he knew it. His father made him play and the only reason he played goal was that he got to spend most of his time on the bench.

It was time for us to go out onto the ice and Finnie still wasn't there; Coach Hunter was about to blow a gasket. "I don't ask much of you boys," he shouted. "All I ask is that you try your best. And that you show up. Now can anyone tell me where the hell Walsh is?"

Of course, no one knew.

We went out onto the ice, without Finnie, and we got slaughtered. After 60 minutes of humiliatingly painful play, we skulked into the dressing room, having lost by a score of 14-2.

We sat there forlornly, waiting for Coach Hunter to come in and chew us out. God knows I wanted him to yell at us. We were terrible out there, every one of us. Tom Kazakoff was the worst, without a doubt, but the rest of us were pretty bad, too. We deserved to lose that game.

But Coach Hunter didn't yell at us. He was mad, for sure. A large vein bulged in the middle of his forehead and he rhythmically clenched and unclenched his fists. "If anyone sees Walsh, tell him he's benched for the rest of the season." He walked out of the dressing room, mercifully leaving us alone with our shame.

I showered, got changed and left the arena. I avoided both my own family as well as Finnie's. As I crossed the parking lot,

I heard someone call my name. I turned and saw Joyce Sweeney running to catch up with me. "Hey Paul," she said, breathing hard. Her face was flushed from the cold.

"Hey," I said. I had never been around Joyce without Finnie. It felt a little weird.

"Where was Finnie tonight?"

"I don't know. He didn't say anything to me about missing the game."

"You guys lost pretty badly."

"Yeah. It was brutal."

There was an uncomfortable pause and I shifted my gaze to the ground, pretending to be very interested in a particular square of pavement.

"So you don't know what happened to Finnie?" she asked finally.

"Nope. I wish I did."

"Me too." She started to leave, then turned back. "When you see Finnie, tell him I said hi."

"Sure," I said, a little disappointed.

Joyce walked off in the direction of the arena. I watched her until she disappeared, then continued across the parking lot. I didn't know what was wrong with Finnie, but I had an idea where he was. I jogged to the sawmill and, picking my way along the dark trail, negotiated my way to the reservoir.

We hadn't made a rink that year. What with school and our fairly busy city league hockey schedule, we just hadn't had the time.

I found Finnie in what would have been the goal crease. He had lit a fire and was tossing his hockey card collection into it, one card at a time. "Hey Finnie," I said, sitting down.

"Hey Paul."

"Where were you tonight?"

He didn't answer me.

"Remember, the game? Coach Hunter is mad as hell at you."
He still didn't say anything.

"We got shellacked."

He shifted his attention from the fire to me. "Pelle Lindbergh is dead," he said. He continued to flip his cards into the fire. He refused to say anything more.

Pelle Lindbergh had been out celebrating a win over the Boston Bruins with the rest of the Philadelphia Flyers the preceding Saturday night when, driving home, he lost control of his car and slammed into a wall. Suffering from severe spinal cord and brain injuries, a fractured skull and broken legs, he was pronounced brain dead at the hospital. After two days, his family requested that the life support be turned off and his organs removed for donation. Pelle Lindbergh was 26 years old. His blood-alcohol level was 0.24 percent.

Lindbergh's death had a marked impact on Finnie. He no longer displayed any interest in professional hockey; when Wayne Gretzky and the Edmonton Oilers were eliminated in the second-round playoffs that year, he didn't say a word. What was more astonishing was that he refused to have anything to do with a rookie goaltender, Patrick Roy, who led the Montreal Canadiens to the Stanley Cup that year. Even when Peter Stastny and the Quebec Nordiques finished first in their division, he remained silent. Stastny had 122 points that year, the league's sixth-best total. Gretzky had 215 points, the highest of his career.

At the next practice, Finnie played horribly but didn't seem to care. It wasn't until after practice, in the locker room, that I noticed what he had done to his jersey. He had unstitched and reversed his old number, Pelle Lindbergh's number, from a 31 to a 13. Lindbergh had died on the 13th of November, Finnie's 13th birthday. I don't know if Finnie switched the number to pay homage to Lindbergh or as some ominous symbolic gesture and

I didn't ask him. I'm not sure I wanted to know.

Coach Hunter stuck to his guns regarding Finnie's benching. Maybe if Finnie had played better in practice he would have been more willing to go back on his decision. As it was, Coach Hunter had no choice but to back up his threat. He had, after all, announced Finnie's punishment in front of the entire team. Team discipline would have almost certainly suffered and we needed all the discipline we could get with Tom Kazakoff between the pipes. So it was settled; Finnie would ride the pine for the rest of the season.

Tom Kazakoff was as disappointed with Coach Hunter's decision as the rest of us, if not more. He was physically ill before every game and sometimes again between periods. Once he even begged Finnie to switch jerseys and equipment with him and take his place on the ice. He hated playing and, if his father hadn't been so determined his son would become an NHL star, would have quit instantly. By the end of the season, we had lost all but five games and, of the five, two were ties and one we won because the other team forfeited.

With Finnie out, and such a poor goaltender in his place, it was my turn to shine. Defence suddenly became our top priority and, since I was the most defensive of our defencemen, I got plenty of ice time.

What I gained in skill Finnie lost. Finnie had always been a hefty kid and would probably have been overweight if he wasn't constantly wearing his goalie equipment and playing hockey. When Pelle Lindbergh died and Finnie got benched, he stopped wearing his equipment and stopped playing except in practice, where he put in little to no effort. He began to gain weight. He began to slow down.

I first noticed it when he came back from Christmas vacation. Mr. Walsh took Finnie and his brothers to Hawaii for the holidays, so I didn't see him for nearly three weeks. I was shocked. His once-solid frame had softened and his face was much rounder. At the age of 13, Finnie had what looked to be a beer belly.

I suspected that Finnie's lethargic lifestyle was causing the decline in his physique. Since there was absolutely no chance of Coach Hunter changing his mind, there was only one option. I would have to rebuild the rink.

The problem was that, unlike Finnie, I didn't have access to the supplies. The boards were rotten and our hose and squeegee were gone. I would need Finnie's help.

"No way," he said when I proposed the idea.

"Why not?"

"I don't *want* to play anymore."

"Come on, Finnie. This is a good idea."

"No, it's not. Look, I know what you're trying to do, but it won't work. I just don't care anymore. There's no point to it."

"It'll toughen us up," I said.

"Big deal."

♦

Years later, when I was told the details, I realized that Finnie's obsessive desire to be stronger, faster and tougher was a direct result of his mother's death, an incident that Finnie was far too young to even remember.

Driving home from the hospital after Finnie's birth, Mr. Walsh, Mrs. Walsh and Finnie were sideswiped by a transport truck carrying a load of hiking boots. Their car spun out of control and they careened down an embankment and onto the frozen river. It was late November and the river was covered with a shroud of ice, but the impact cracked it. Roger Walsh was stunned, though basically unharmed, but Finnie's mother sustained serious injuries, not the least of which were two broken legs.

She was unable to leave the car under her own power and when Roger Walsh attempted to free her she insisted that he first take Finnie to safety. Finnie, due to good fortune and the experience of a woman who had already raised three children well into boyhood, was securely strapped into a car seat in the back. Roger Walsh did what his wife told him; she was always more clearheaded in times of crisis than he was and he had learned to listen to her. He freed a tiny, screaming Finnie from the car seat and scrambled along the ice, slipping several times, until he got to the riverbank. He wrapped Finnie in his sweater and placed him in a snowbank, then went back for his wife. He moved as fast as he could, but he was not a man accustomed to extreme physical activity. As he returned to the car, the ice creaked and cracked; Roger Walsh feared that it would break. He had read somewhere that when you're on cracked ice you should lie on your stomach and crawl across it, dispersing your weight and lessening the stress on the ice.

Roger Walsh crawled along the ice as fast as he could, flinching as it crackled, the sound reminding him of the time his grandfather had taken him hunting but had been forced to bring him home in tears, young Roger having been terrified by the sound of the rifle. Just as Roger Walsh got to the car, the ice gave way and the car slid into the river, the trunk disappearing and then the back doors and then the front doors and windshield and then the hood and finally the headlights, their faint light disappearing beneath the surface. Roger Walsh saw his wife's eyes one last time just before she went under. At that moment help arrived from several motorists who had seen the accident. But, despite the heroic efforts of several men who risked their own lives and dove beneath the frozen surface, Mrs. Walsh could not be saved. Roger Walsh never really got over the feeling that maybe, if he had been a little faster, a little stronger, a little tougher, he could have saved his wife.

Finnie had inherited that feeling. From a very early age, he knew that he must be ready at all times, because disaster can strike at any moment. In his estimation goalies were the epitome of toughness and Pelle Lindbergh was the best of the lot. But, as tough and strong and fast as Lindbergh undeniably was, he still died a senseless death. It destroyed the way Finnie looked at the world.

The only other person who recognized that something was wrong with Finnie was Sarah. She set her mind to finding out what it was. "Why are you sad?" she asked him. It was April of 1986, five months after Pelle Lindbergh's death, and our horrible season had finally ended. Sarah had just turned four.

"I'm not sad, Sarah," Finnie said. He tried his best to keep his problems to himself when he was around her.

"What are you then?"

"I'm not anything. I'm Finnie."

"No. What are you?"

"I'm nothing. I'm fine. Do you want some juice?" Juice usually worked when it came to distracting Sarah, but she was onto us and only let it work when she had nothing to lose.

"No. You're sad."

"All right, maybe I'm a little sad."

"Why?"

"Because someone died."

"Who died?"

"A hockey player."

"Was he your friend?"

"No, I didn't know him."

"Then why are you sad?"

"I don't know. I just am."

"Why?"

"I don't know. Really."

Sarah was puzzled by this. As far as she was concerned, Finnie always had the answers. That night Finnie was going to stay for supper, but when we sat down at the table he was nowhere to be found.

"Where's Finnie?" my mother asked.

"I guess he went home," I said.

"He's sad," Sarah said.

"What's wrong with him?" asked my father.

"A hockey player died," Sarah answered.

My father's eyebrows dropped. "He's still upset about Pelle Lindbergh?"

"Yeah," I said.

"But that was over five months ago."

"I know, but he was Finnie's hero."

"Finnie's put on a lot of weight," my mother said.

"He won't play hockey anymore," I said.

"Because your coach benched him?"

"Not just that. He doesn't even try in practice." I didn't tell them about the reservoir rink and his refusal to rebuild it.

"Finnie doesn't try?" My father's mouth hung open, full of food.

"No."

"What do you mean?"

"I mean he doesn't care. He didn't care that Coach Hunter benched him."

"That's not like Finnie," my mother said.

"Damn right it's not," my father said.

"He has been acting strange lately."

"I can't believe he's not trying."

"And he has put on all that weight."

"Someone had better have a talk with that boy."

I wondered what good it would do; rocks weren't going to work on Finnie this time.

One evening several days later, Finnie and I were sitting in the kitchen watching Sarah for my mother, who had a headache and wanted to lie down for a while, when my father came in and invited us to join him on the back deck. We went outside and Sarah ran to play on the tire swing my father had built for her. It was unusual for her to leave us alone like that when there was obviously going to be a conversation. I knew then that it was a setup.

My father wasted no time. "I hear you've lost interest in hockey, Finnie."

"I guess I have," Finnie answered, looking at me suspiciously. "It just isn't what it used to be."

"Because of Pelle Lindbergh?"

"Sort of. It's bigger than that, though. Because what happened to Pelle Lindbergh can happen to anyone."

"You mean dying?"

"No, it's the way he died. Needlessly," he looked at me, "like Bill Barilko."

"I don't know if I agree with that, Finnie," my father said. "Death is death. Sometimes a death has a purpose, but most of the time people just die."

"I know."

"On the other hand, there's Georges Vezina to consider."

"Who?"

"Georges Vezina, the Chicoutimi Cucumber, the Silent Habitant. He was a goalie for the Montreal Canadiens in the first part of the century, back when goalies had to stay on their feet to make saves. He was the father of 22 children and won two Stanley Cups, once stopping 78 shots in one game. The Vezina Trophy for the most valuable goaltender, which I believe your boy Pelle Lindbergh won last season, is named after him."

"Yeah. Lot of good the Vezina did Lindbergh."

"I'm not finished, Finnie. They called him the Chicoutimi

Cucumber because he was as cool as a cucumber, or so the saying goes. They called him the Silent Habitant because he never, ever complained, which for a Frenchman is indeed a noteworthy feat.

"One night in November of 1925, Montreal was playing Pittsburgh. After the first period, having shut out Pittsburgh magnificently, Vezina left the ice bleeding from his mouth, even though no one remembered him having been hit with the puck. He collapsed in the dressing room during the intermission, but pulled himself together and started the second period. He made it through most of the period, but then he collapsed again. Four months later he died of tuberculosis. He had told no one, not even his family, that he was mortally ill. But he left that last game without having let a goal in. He went out with a shutout. He went out on a high note."

Finnie was speechless.

"Lindbergh, he was a good goalie, right?" my father asked.

"He was one of the best," Finnie said.

"But there's more to it than that, right? Well, the rest of it is what makes the difference, Finnie. That's what matters."

After that, Finnie's attitude toward hockey changed: it was more than a game, about more than stopping pucks, although that would always be his foremost concern. To Finnie hockey was about life and death and about every other player who had ever lived and died. It was a religion.

Once Finnie got his legs back, he was a far better goalie than he'd been before Pelle Lindbergh died, which was pretty damn good. The difference was that now he was playing for himself.

◆

In the middle of 1987, my father finished reading every *National Geographic* ever printed and was reduced from a pace of three issues a week to one a month. At first he enjoyed the extra free time, but then he began to get restless. My mother and Louise and I grew nervous; unlike Sarah, we remembered the week he had spent saving us from the garage. We knew it was only a matter of time before he found something else to occupy his time. The possibilities were frightening.

His only friend, Pal, was not the most stable influence we could have hoped for. His prosthetic arms had been disappearing fairly steadily over the years and at that point I believe he had gone through over 20 arms. We didn't know whether he lost the arms or whether they were stolen; to be honest, I don't think Pal knew either. What possible use would anyone else have for them? There was just no motive.

I thought that perhaps Pal was losing them on purpose, but Louise didn't think so; if he didn't want them, then why did he keep getting more? Sarah thought that maybe they were running away on their own, like the dish and the spoon, off to find their true loves, a sort of prosthetic-limb *Romeo and Juliet*. My mother didn't know what to think. My father supported a wide array of theories, some completely bizarre, but he always believed Pal when he said he was sure he hadn't just misplaced a claw. Not even one of the 20 arms had been recovered.

The range of hobbies available to a one-armed man is somewhat limited. Generally speaking, my father was drawn to cerebral activities rather than physical ones. He did not work well in groups and, with the exception of Mr. Palagopolis, did not seem to enjoy the company of other people. He hadn't always been this way; before the accident he was a very sociable man, with many friends and interests. After he lost his arm, however, my father became reclusive. His exile was self-imposed, for reasons known only to him. It became more noticeable with each passing year.

Strangely enough, the more my father shuttered himself away, the more Louise ventured out. It was as if there was something in our house, something very precious and very valuable, that the two of them were responsible for guarding. Apparently they took shifts; Louise's shift had lasted for the first decade or so of her life and it was time now for my father to take over the task.

At the age of 17, Louise was making the most of her new-found freedom. What she had lacked in popularity and social poise when she was younger she made up for as a teen. She was in grade 12, her last year of high school, and she was one of the most well-liked and romantically pursued girls in school. Whereas before she had been completely incapable of conversation, she was now well respected and frequently sought after for advice. I unexpectedly found myself in the position of being known not as Paul Woodward the grade 10 student, or Paul Woodward the hockey player, or even just plain Paul Woodward, but as what's his name, Louise Woodward's little brother.

It's hard to say what finally prompted Louise to make the leap. It was a normal day and Finnie, Sarah and I were sitting at the kitchen table playing Monopoly or some other stupid board game in which none of us had any real interest. This wasn't long after Finnie had decided to play hockey again. It was raining outside, not hard, but hard enough to make us want to stay inside and Louise had been down in the basement by herself all afternoon doing whatever it was she did down there.

I was getting frustrated with Sarah, because she kept forgetting how to play the game. Finnie, by far the more patient of the two of us, and indeed one of the most patient people I have ever known, explained the rules to her again and again and again and still she would forget. Maybe she didn't; maybe she just enjoyed listening to Finnie, I don't know. Either way she was really annoying me, so I was just about to quit when Louise stomped up the stairs carrying a large cardboard box.

She plopped the box onto the table, upsetting our game and sending pieces careening onto the floor. "Here, Sarah, you can have this if you want," she said.

"What is it?" Sarah asked, already clamouring to open the box.

"A bunch of useless junk." Louise walked to the front door.

Finnie and I followed her, watching speechlessly as she put on her shoes and coat and opened the door.

"Where are you going?" I asked her.

"Outside, I guess."

"It's raining."

"Yes, I can see that, Paul."

"Do you want us to come?" Finnie asked.

"No, that's okay. I've got a lot of stuff to do."

Louise left and we went back into the kitchen. I thought the whole thing was a bit weird, but then I looked over at Finnie and saw that he was smiling. I asked him what he was smiling about.

"You'll see," he said.

Sarah was standing on the table wrestling with the lid of the box. Finnie laughed when he saw what was inside; I was shocked. Sarah was delighted; she had never been allowed to play with Louise's toys before and as a result they were all in mint condition. Sarah had a tendency to be very hard on her belongings. She usually broke or wore out anything she was given within a matter of weeks, but Louise had kept the same stuff forever. I knew that if Louise had given her things to Sarah, then she had to be serious about abandoning them; she'd never get anything back in one piece.

Once freed, Louise was like a snowball rolling down a hill. It was only a matter of months before she had more friends than anyone I knew. She always had something to do, was always going somewhere. Finnie and I became nothing more than members of her ever-growing crowd.

In his own right, Finnie had also ascended to a position of social success. This was partly due to his last name, partly because he was genuinely a nice guy. He would go out of his way to help a friend and he never pushed anybody around. He could easily have been a bully; at 15 he was at least six inches taller than anyone else in our grade and he had girth as well as height. He had always been heavy-set, even overweight at times, but when he worked at it he commanded attention.

Finnie was one of those rare guys who, in junior high school, was realistically in a position to consider dating older girls. But Finnie rarely had girlfriends and seemed to be indifferent to the advances of girls regardless of their age or appearance.

I'm sure that a good deal of his appeal came from his prowess as a goaltender. Since the end of that awful season when Tom Kazakoff had been in net, Finnie had consistently been the best goalie in our league and every year more and more people came out to see our games, motivated by the prospect of seeing yet another stellar performance between the pipes by the one and only Finnie Walsh.

I was progressing too, but as a defenceman I was the object of far less attention. People only notice defencemen when they screw up and, since I screwed up more rarely than the other defencemen on our team, I was noticed less by the fans. The opposing teams' coaches and players knew about me, though; more than once I was marked for an especially brutal check, a spear, a slash or even challenged to a fight. Thanks to Gerry and Kirby Walsh, I was used to this kind of abuse and had ways of dealing with it. Finnie would get really mad when he saw players go after me and more than once he got tossed out of a game for charging a player who'd made me the victim of a dirty play. He wielded his stick like a scythe, terrifying offending players, though he never actually hit anyone. This only served to increase

Finnie's popularity with both sexes; nothing was as attractive as skill and unpredictability.

Even my father started coming to games on a regular basis. He bought one of those big foam hands, the ones with the index finger pointing straight up, and attached it to the stump of his missing arm. He thought it was hilarious, as did Sarah, but my mother and Louise thought it was morbid and more than a bit creepy. My father had been wearing it for a while when, during a game, Finnie made an absolutely spectacular save in the dying seconds of a tied game. The crowd was on their feet as the buzzer sounded, eagerly awaiting a period of overtime. As we skated toward the bench, I saw Finnie look into the stands and drop his glove, stick and blocker. My father was standing on his seat, cheering wildly, pointing his giant foam finger at Finnie.

It had been almost seven years since the accident and by then I had pretty much come to terms with any lingering feelings of guilt, but I could see by the look on Finnie's face that he had not. I skated up to him and pushed him across the ice to the bench. By the time play resumed, he had managed to partially recover, but he was still shaken.

Finnie let in the first shot he faced, a slow floater high on his glove side, and we lost the game. No one said much to Finnie about it; what could they say? Finnie lost us the game, but without him it would have been lost long before that. He didn't want to talk after the game and the next day he seemed to be back to normal, so I didn't belabour the issue. Finnie appeared to have bounced back. Tom Kazakoff was very much relieved.

As far as I know, my father, usually very perceptive where such things were concerned, had no idea of the effect that he and his foam finger had on Finnie. By then he seemed to be pretty much oblivious to anything that wasn't directly related to Mr. Palagopolis' missing arms. Apparently this was to be his new hobby: the tracking down and recovery of Pal's missing limbs. He bought a 1940s detective hat and wore it almost constantly, which irritated my mother, who thought he looked stupid. She was right, he did look kind of goofy, but my father ignored her pleas; he had more important things on his mind.

He made a large chart that chronicled the disappearance of all the claws, recording as much information as Pal could remember, and he noticed a pattern. Most of the claws went missing during school hours, when Mr. Palagopolis was working as a janitor. As a precaution against the loss of further arms, my father made Pal promise not to take his arm off at school. This would prove to be a nearly impossible task; he was constantly taking the arm off and putting it on, out of nervousness.

For some reason, Pal seemed older when he wasn't wearing his arm, but almost childlike when he was. When he strapped on his claw, it was almost as if he went back in time to the way he had been before the war. It had been over 40 years since Pal had lost his real arm; he should have adjusted to it by now. After all, he had been without his arm for almost twice as long as he had been with it.

To prevent the claw from being stolen when Pal wasn't wearing it, my father drilled a hole in the plastic frame of the arm. He gave Pal my old bicycle lock so when Pal took off his arm, he could thread the lock through the hole and lock it to something solid. The only problem with this strategy was that Pal kept forgetting the combination, as did my father. I asked my father to write the combination down, but he refused, saying that the information was safer if it was committed to memory. He tried his best to remember the combination, but he never could, and neither could Pal.

Mr. Palagopolis' workroom in the basement of the school was a jumble of mops and brooms and buckets and rags. It was really no wonder things had a way of going missing; for all we knew it could contain a piece of Amelia Earhart's plane, Jimmy Hoffa's

Steven Galloway

body, even a Sasquatch or two. Therefore, when Pal excitedly telephoned my father one afternoon from the school and told him
that his claw had been stolen again, my father asked him if he
was *absolutely* sure.

"Of course, Bob. You know your mess and I know my mess. My
claw is snatched again," answered Pal.

My father immediately put on his hat and went down to the
school to investigate. He found Pal in the hallway trying to mop
the floor.

"I tell you, I've just about had it," Pal said. "I treat them right,
am nice to them, and still they go away. I've just about had it for
sure."

My father asked Pal if he had remembered to lock up the
claw, which he said he had.

"Well, how did it get away then?"

"I don't know. The lock was open and my claw was gone.
That's all I know."

Apparently, Pal had been in the workroom eating his lunch
and when he'd finished he'd gone to use the washroom. Pal almost
never took his claw into the washroom; he said that it was too
nasty a thing to put near himself when he was so vulnerable. He
was sure that he had locked it up. He'd been gone for 10 minutes,
maybe 15, and when he'd gotten back the arm was gone.

Pal and my father weren't the only ones who lost something
that week, though. Sarah had found an old yellow life jacket in
the box of stuff that Louise had given to her. She had worn it every
day since then. It had a whistle attached to the front of it, a small
plastic whistle, like a referee's, and more often than not you could
hear Sarah coming long before you saw her, its shrill cry announc-
ing her imminent arrival.

There was something about that whistle; it seemed to have
the ability to cut through every variety of background noise. It

was almost supernatural, which is probably why Sarah liked it.

When it went missing, she was far more upset than I would have expected. Sarah lost things all the time, almost daily, yet nothing had ever upset her like this. Finnie and I were in the driveway, just about to leave for hockey practice, when she came running out the front door.

"It's gone!" There were tears in her eyes.

"What's gone?" I asked.

"My jacket."

"The life jacket?" I asked.

She nodded.

"Well, where did you last have it?"

She thought for a moment. "I don't know."

"You don't know?"

"I had it yesterday."

Finnie, who was always more patient with five-year-old Sarah, put down his equipment bag and took charge of the situation. "Where could it be?" he asked her.

"I looked in my room and it's not there. I looked in the kitchen and it's not there. I looked in the yard and it's not there and I looked in the basement and it's not there."

"Did you ask your dad if he's seen it?"

"He's busy with Mr. Pal today."

They were obviously still in the midst of a far more important investigation.

"I'll tell you what, Sarah. Paul and I have to go to hockey practice now, but we'll come back right after and help you look for it."

"No, no, no, no. I need it now."

"Come on, Sarah. We'll catch hell if we miss practice," I said.

Her hands clenched into fists and she walked up to Finnie. I thought maybe she was going to hit him, but he bent down and she whispered something into his ear that I couldn't hear. Finnie's face instantly adopted a serious expression. Finnie nodded to her and turned to me. "We're going to have to miss practice." There was no point in arguing. Finnie and Sarah were, besides my father, the two most stubborn people I have ever known.

Finnie could get away with missing a practice here and there; he was our star player. The only person who would mind would be Tom Kazakoff and it was just a practice, so he would have had to play anyway. Besides, Coach Hunter was still with our team, having decided to follow the same group of boys through their childhood hockey years and then start at the bottom with a new group of kids. He believed that this particular method of coaching was more personally satisfying, partly because it allowed him to see the progress of the players he coached, partly because it meant that he wouldn't have to learn a new set of names each year. Anyway, Coach Hunter remembered what had happened back in the 1985–86 season when he had benched Finnie and I was sure he didn't want to go through that again, ever. So Finnie was safe.

I knew that I, however, would be punished. If a guy like me was allowed to miss a practice without consequence, then that meant anyone could. Team anarchy would ensue. That's how I figured Coach Hunter would see things. He was preoccupied with preventing breakdown. He had seen it happen once and from what I gathered it wasn't pretty.

As it turned out, I was right about getting punished; at the next practice, I was made to skate from one end of the rink, stop, turn, skate to the other end of the rink, stop, turn and repeat the process for the full two hours. I didn't really mind; I knew that I deserved it. I was a little surprised that Finnie was given the same punishment, though. Coach Hunter made him skate too, and in full equipment. In hindsight, I can see that he didn't really have a choice. He had to punish me, and if he punished me and didn't punish Finnie, for the same offence on the same day, then all hell would break loose. We skated until our legs were on fire and our lungs screamed for oxygen. I never regretted it, though.

Besides being yellow and wearing a life jacket whenever she left the house, Sarah was superstitious, placing great stock in dreams and hunches and omens. I don't know where she got it from; my father was the exact opposite, although he was given to believing in things that were, to say the least, a little out there. My mother was about as sensible and practical as people come and I wasn't any different. I took after our mother, I think, and Louise had more of our father in her. I don't know where Sarah came from.

Sarah's main source of otherworldly information emanated, from of all places, a lamp. She had always been fascinated by light and this source was her favourite. It was on the table beside her bed. The shade was made of bits of different-coloured glass, like stained glass but cheaper, and when you turned out all the other lights it cast a multicoloured pattern on the ceiling. The bolt that held the shade onto the top of the lamp was loose, so you could take the shade and spin it around, creating a sort of kaleidoscopic effect. Every night, before she turned the light out and went to bed, Sarah would give the lamp as hard a spin as her tiny yellow arm could muster and then she would lie back on her bed and search the ceiling for pictures. Ninety-nine percent of the time she saw nothing, but every once in a while there was something there, or so she thought. One of her predictions had already come true.

My mother and father had purchased tickets to a concert. When they were phoning for a babysitter several days before the event, Sarah told them not to bother because my mother would be sick that day. They didn't really pay much attention; Sarah's dislike of babysitters was well known. Sarah preferred Louise, but she had plans that night and I wasn't considered old enough. I was 12 or 13 at the time, so I didn't need a babysitter myself, but

Sarah required so much attention that they didn't want to leave me in charge of her.

When the day of the concert rolled around, my mother was too busy retching her insides out, the latest victim of a stomach flu, to care whether Sarah had been right or not. They hadn't needed that babysitter, just as Sarah had predicted. Of course, it's possible that it was all just a coincidence.

It didn't take us long to find Sarah's life jacket. It was sitting on the back porch, beside the pile of *National Geographics*. Sarah was beside herself with joy, immediately putting it on, zipping it up and running around the yard, blowing excitedly on the shrill whistle. The fact that it was several sizes too large didn't bother her in the least; she knew that she would grow into it.

At first I was upset that we had missed practice for what appeared to be nothing more than Sarah's forgetfulness. Then Finnie told me what she had whispered to him. She'd told Finnie that the lamp had conveyed a message: she would *drown*. That was why she wore the life jacket. Sarah, stubborn as she was, had found a way to cheat death. It never occurred to her to question the reliability of the lamp. She had a problem and, with the discovery of the life jacket, a solution.

Finnie made me promise not to tell anyone else about Sarah's premonition. Finnie's mother had drowned and I imagined that he had similar fears. Maybe he even had a life jacket or two of his own stowed away somewhere.

Meanwhile, Roger Walsh's own fears were fast being realized. Of his four sons, Finnie was the only one not currently charged with some sort of offence and was whole of mind and body. Patrick Walsh, 23 years old, who had once so proudly announced his intention to enter the pornographic film industry, had apparently decided that gratuitous sex wasn't enough, so he turned to drugs and booze. Roger sent him to Calgary to scout out a possible business deal, hoping that a little responsibility would force Pat to grow up. He liked Calgary a lot, or so he told Roger, and even though the business deal didn't pan out, Patrick decided to move there and make a fresh start. In the middle of January he was found wandering naked through downtown Calgary, drunk or stoned or both. He lost three of his toes and the tips of his ears to frostbite. Upon investigation the police in Calgary discovered that Patrick had been dealing narcotics and charged him with a variety of criminal offences.

The next eldest son, Gerry, was involved in a drunken high-speed chase with police through the streets of Toronto, where he had been attending university. Roger had pulled some strings with his *alma mater* to get Gerry admitted and even more to keep him enrolled after two disastrous years, but this time there was nothing he could do. Gerry was at home now, having broken both of his legs and his collarbone in the crash that directly followed the chase. He had a court date set in a month's time.

Kirby, the youngest of Roger Walsh's sons to remember his mother, had always been the wildest. After graduating from high school, Kirby bought a car and embarked upon a year-long road trip. The family got the occasional postcard, but Kirby never said much. The only real contact Roger had with him was his once-a-month visit to the bank to put money into his account. He could have asked his business manager to do it, but Roger did it himself because it was the best way to keep from forgetting Kirby entirely. Even after Kirby crippled a man in a bar fight in New Orleans, receiving four years in jail for his efforts, Roger went to the bank each month, depositing money into an account that would not be withdrawn from for years to come.

Kirby's incarceration didn't surprise Finnie in the least. Of his brothers, Kirby had always been the most vicious. "He's like some sort of fucked-up, sadistic hobo," Finnie said when Kirby first left.

"Who?"

"Kirby doesn't know when to stop. He has *never* known when to stop."

"Watch out for Ahab," I said.

"Ahab nothing. Kirby had better watch out for that whale. The whale wins in the end."

Finnie was far closer to the members of my family, especially Louise and Sarah, than he was to his own. Having no sisters himself, he treated the girls better than any real brother would have; there was none of the sibling rivalry or petty bickering or ordinary fighting that brothers and sisters are famous for. He set awfully high standards for me and I'll admit that if either Sarah or Louise had been made to choose, they'd have chosen him every day of the week and they would have been right.

With Sarah, Finnie was very protective, almost mothering. He somehow managed to do this in a manner that didn't upset her. There were times when Finnie and Sarah reminded me, strange as this may sound, of an old married couple, their relationship rich in secret jokes and sideways glances. I suppose that all of us were like that with Sarah to some extent; it was hard not to be. How could you *not* love that little yellow girl?

Finnie's relationship with Louise was different. Finnie had always been the only one of us to know, even to some small degree, what was going on inside her head. Louise was hard to get truly close to, but Finnie broke through.

♦

It was a standard high school bush party. There was a bonfire, sloppy teenage drunkenness, car stereos blasting. Thanks to Finnie's social status and the fact that I was Louise Woodward's younger brother, Finnie and I were allowed to attend it even though we were lowly 10th graders.

Finnie and I each drank a couple of beers, both to fit in and because we had quite recently developed a taste for it. We stood around the bonfire watching people drag piece after piece of wood out of the brush and pile it on the already well-fuelled fire. Several times we were forced to talk a drunken Jim Stockdale out of running through it. Both Jim Stockdale and Frank Hawthorne had been held back so they were high school seniors in the envious position of being old enough to buy liquor. Louise was seeing Frank Hawthorne at the time, behind my father's back of course.

I was beginning to feel a buzz and had just settled in to enjoy it when Jim Stockdale, who couldn't have feathered one of his picture-perfect passes I remembered so well to save his life, decided that reason was in fact *not* the better part of valour and made a lunge for the fire. I reacted by tackling him, but he was strong and I had a hell of a time holding him down. Finnie ran off to find Frank Hawthorne.

Jim's pyrotropic tendencies were a regular occurrence at these bush parties. His house burned down when Jim was four years old and although no one was hurt something screwy happened to his mind between the time the fire broke out and the moment Mr. Stockdale pulled him out of the house by the scruff of his neck. The part of the story that no one ever mentioned, and that neither Finnie nor I would have known if my father hadn't told us, was that Jim didn't want to leave the house. For a while people speculated that Jim had been responsible for the fire, a contention unsupported by the fire department investigators, who said that it had been the result of faulty wiring and insulation that had not been manufactured to code.

Whatever the deep-seated psychological reason behind Jim Stockdale's urge to run through the bonfire, if indeed there was one beyond the fact that he was a drunken idiot, it was common knowledge that Frank Hawthorne was the only person who could talk him out of it. As I held onto Jim, my arms wrapped securely around his legs, I hoped that Frank was somewhere close at hand and that Finnie would find him quickly.

Finnie did not return quickly, but someone else grabbed Jim's arms and helped to hold him down. A few moments later there were sounds of a scuffle behind us. Someone yelled that a fight had broken out and everybody, including Jim, strained to see who was involved. Reasonably assured that Jim was no longer interested in running through the fire, I let go of his legs and jogged over to investigate the commotion.

A crowd was gathered on the edge of the clearing, where several cars were parked haphazardly. At first I couldn't see, so I climbed up onto the bed of a pickup to get a better view.

The crowd had made a circle and contained within it were Frank Hawthorne and Finnie. Off to the side I saw Louise, crying, clutching her shoulder where her shirt was torn. Frank looked pretty drunk, judging from the way he was moving, and Finnie was bleeding from his lip. Frank had every conceivable advantage; he was older, bigger, stronger and the crowd was on his side. Finnie seemed to be holding his own, though, and although it was rumoured that Frank carried a knife there was no sign of any weapon.

This was not a hockey fight, nor was it like a fight on TV. Both Frank's and Finnie's eyes were bright with anger and their blows were wild and uncalculated. Finnie tagged Frank with a hard left and Frank looked like he might go down, but he recovered at the last second and caught Finnie solidly in the stomach. Finnie doubled over and Frank wrapped his arm around Finnie's neck in a headlock and began feeding Finnie punches. It looked like Finnie was beaten.

I tried to work my way to the front of the crowd, pushing people aside as fast as I could. As I reached the front of the mêlée, Finnie, nose broken, lips bloody and swollen, both eyes blackened and swelling shut, still did not concede defeat. With Frank raining blows upon him, Finnie wrapped his arms around Frank's legs, picked Frank up off the ground and began to spin him around. With an almost superhuman heave, he threw Frank over his head into the mass of people. There were cries of surprise from the people Frank landed on, then a hush from all but two people.

One was Jennifer Carlysle, a plain-looking girl in the 11th grade. I didn't know her very well; she was shy and quiet and I was surprised to even see her at the party. As far as I knew, she didn't usually go to these sorts of things. It turned out that this party was her first, having been coerced into coming by her boyfriend, Marty, Tom Kazakoff's cousin. She was crying hysterically because Frank had landed squarely on top of her and her thumb had been broken. She didn't know it was broken until almost a week later, when she finally went to the hospital. Marty kept telling her that it was fine, that she was just being a baby. She made the mistake of believing him and as a result her thumb never set properly and remained crooked for the rest of her life, as far as I know. I think she broke up with Marty after that.

The other person making noise was Frank Hawthorne. He was shrieking like a wounded animal, clutching his face and rolling around on the ground. Between Frank and Jennifer there was quite a ruckus going on, so I suppose that someone must have called the police or gone for help when it became clear what had happened. The police called an ambulance and after the attendants took Frank away they rooted through the trampled grass where Frank had landed. Eventually the beams from their flashlights located Frank's left eye. It was sitting in the middle of a leaf, like an hors d'oeuvre on a napkin, unmoved from where it had landed after Jennifer Carlysle's thumb had cleanly disgorged it from its socket.

Because Frank had thrown the first punch and because Finnie was a minor, the police didn't press charges, but Frank's family sued Finnie's dad, who settled out of court for what was a considerable sum if you were a member of the Hawthorne family, but a pittance if your last name was Walsh.

Neither Finnie nor Louise nor Frank ever publicly discussed the cause of the fight. I don't know all the details, but I do know that Finnie arrived just in time. I would have known that anyway; Finnie *always* arrived just in time.

◆

Not long after Finnie's father gave the Hawthornes a ton of money for Frank's eye, Joyce Sweeney and Finnie started dating. It was weird, to say the least. She had only gotten better as she'd grown older; to this day I still think she is one of the most beautiful women I've ever met. She had a way of making you feel completely at ease. You wanted to touch her, not necessarily in a sexual way, more like you would a dog or a cat. Joyce was a real catch, that much was obvious. I was happy for Finnie.

His fight with Frank Hawthorne changed the way many people looked at Finnie; he became the villain. Whereas before he was known as a mild-mannered, easygoing guy, after the fight people began to treat him like a time bomb. It didn't matter that there had been obvious extenuating circumstances behind the altercation; Finnie was a rich kid who had blinded a poor kid in a fight. This really bothered Finnie; he'd always been sensitive about his family's money and relied heavily on the acceptance of his peers to bolster his self-esteem. When kids avoided him in the halls at school, I think a part of him believed they were right.

While Finnie was struggling with his new image, my father and Mr. Palagopolis were busy battling the person they now only half-jokingly called the "one-arm bandit." Pal had recently received claw number 22. After the last incident, both my father and Pal were more determined than ever to defeat their nemesis.

Their plan was to adapt the system making slight modifications. Whenever Pal took off the arm, he was to lock it up with my old bike lock, but he was no longer allowed to take it off at the school. Pal complained bitterly about this; he hated eating with the thing on and he hated going to the washroom with it on and he hated smoking with it on. Once he accidentally pinched his nose in the talons of the claw when he tried to retrieve his cigarette from his mouth.

It was smoking that made him a spectacle; he was eventually unable to smoke outdoors. One day in early January of 1988, he was outside the school enjoying a cigarette, his claw securely chained around a lamp post. He was still wearing the claw; he had only chained it up so he could smoke without fear of hurting himself. Unfortunately, some clever eighth graders discovered this made him the perfect target for snowballs. They pelted him with their icy missiles until he fell to the ground, his eyes wide with fear, unable to defend himself, unable to escape. I remembered that New Year's Eve in 1981 when Pal had besieged us with snowballs and thought it strange that he didn't fight back, but for some reason he seemed incapable of mounting a counter offensive. I think he was too surprised by the swiftness of their assault and the absurdity of his situation to even consider fighting back. The whole ordeal so flustered him that I was called over the PA system to the principal's office. I had to go outside to undo the lock because Pal was too shaken up to remember the combination.

After that, Pal refused to smoke outside and I didn't blame him. Pal never identified his attackers. A few days later, however, a number of eighth-grade students arrived at school and found two things: someone had glued their locks permanently shut with superglue and Mr. Palagopolis, the only person on school grounds who possessed a pair of bolt cutters, was a very busy man. There was no telling when he might have time to cut their locks off.

Sadly this small victory was short-lived. One fine wintry February afternoon, Pal was feeling a bit under the weather. He decided to take a quick nap on the couch in the janitor's room. Fearing both my father's reprimand and an ambush from the claw, Pal locked it to the leg of the couch and settled in for a short rest. When he awoke, feeling much refreshed, the claw was gone. The lock was there, undisturbed, but there was no disputing the fact that the one-arm bandit had struck again.

My father was livid. He combed every inch of the room for clues, talked to people whom he thought might have seen something and questioned Pal over and over again. Pal's response was always the same. "I went to sleep and I wake up and the claw is gone. How it happens I have no ideas. I am asleep."

That night at supper my father was in a particularly foul mood. "I just don't understand it," he said. "Why would anyone want someone else's arm?"

"Maybe they need it," Sarah chirped.

"For what?" I asked.

"I don't know. Maybe they just *think* they need it."

"Could you make any less sense?" Louise asked.

"Probably," Sarah said.

"Why does he keep getting the arms replaced? That's what I don't understand," my mother said.

"Because if he didn't the one-arm bandit would win," I said.

"But he doesn't even like them."

"That's not the point, Mary," my father said. "Someone somewhere doesn't want Pal to have those claws and if he stops replacing them, he admits that he's been beaten. You can't do that."

"I don't see why not. It's just a piece of metal and plastic."

"It's a lot more than that. It's his arm."

To my father and others, the claw was more than an object. I think that every time the one-arm bandit struck, my father relived the trauma of losing his arm. A part of him believed that if he could track down the one-arm bandit, he might recover his own arm.

While my father wanted his arm back, Pal wanted his arm to stay away. He clung to the stubborn conviction that the claw was out to get him. Their search for the one-arm bandit was, in some bizarre way, parallelled by their attempts to heal themselves.

♦

On August 9, 1988, the sport of hockey changed forever. Peter Pocklington, the owner of the Edmonton Oilers, traded Wayne Gretzky, Marty McSorley and Mike Krushelnyski to the Los Angeles Kings in exchange for Jimmy Carson, Martin Gelinas, three first-round draft picks and an estimated $20 million. He sold Wayne Gretzky, the Great One, the most talented hockey player in the history of the game. He sold him like a pair of shoes, a used car or a piece of furniture. I was shattered.

Even Finnie, who had never much liked Gretzky, was angered by the news. "It's like the day the music died," he said.

"What?" I wasn't in the mood for one of Finnie's riddles.

"You know, that song 'American Pie.' About the plane that went down with Buddy Holly and those other two guys on board and rock and roll was changed forever."

"It's not like that."

"Why not?"

"Gretzky's not dead."

"Not *physically*, but he might as well be. He'll never win the cup again. Not in Los Angeles. They don't even have *ice* in Los Angeles."

"Yes, they do."

"No, they don't. It doesn't even get cold in the winter. It's like a fucking tropical island."

"They have ice in the arena."

"That's not the same thing. How can you love hockey if you've never played it? How can you play it if there's no winter? If there's no ice? How can you be a great hockey player in a place where people don't love hockey?"

"That's not even the worst part of it," he continued. "The worst part of it is that it doesn't even matter *where* he plays, where anyone plays, anymore, not now. They're just commodities. They may as well be impaled on rods and put onto a foosball table. There's no magic anymore. You can't own magic. And when you buy it or sell it, it disappears."

"Players get traded all the time, Finnie."

"Yeah, but players don't get *sold* all the time. Not players like Gretzky. What's the point of being as good as he is if you can still be bought and sold? Is it just about money?"

"So what if it is? Money makes the world go around."

"No, it doesn't. That can't be what hockey's about. Hockey is about Georges Vezina and Bill Barilko and Peter Stastny and people playing a game because it's part of who they are."

After the Gretzky trade, Finnie started to dislike the United States. It's true that almost all Canadians share an inherent mistrust of their neighbours to the south and I think that in most cases it's justified because, let's face it, America is nearly always up to something. Finnie, however, was much more adamant about his anti-Americanism than the rest of us. He once remarked that the Gretzky trade was either the day the United States started to buy Canada, piece by piece, or the day it completed the purchase.

That summer Louise and Joyce graduated from high school. Joyce was planning to go to McGill in the fall, but Louise wasn't planning anything. Her marks were good enough to get into any university in the country, but she didn't want to leave. She said that she would go eventually, when she felt she was ready, but until then she was staying in Portsmouth. She got a job as a cashier at the grocery store and my parents were more than pleased when she offered to pay her own expenses.

Although Louise was still the subject of a good deal of attention, she no longer went out on dates. She hadn't since that night Jennifer Carlysle poked Frank Hawthorne's eye out. She still went out with her friends, in groups, to parties, but she was a far cry from the Louise of days gone by. I was actually relieved; it's very traumatic to have your sister go out with guys you know. Sometimes, though, an expression of agonizing sadness faded across Louise's face and I wondered what could possibly be causing her so much trouble and why she didn't do something about it.

It was hard to worry too much about Louise, who handled her problems quietly and independently, when there was Sarah, who handled hers loudly and required as much help as possible.

We were interrupted one lazy morning in late August by screams from Sarah's bedroom. Both my mother and I came running and when we got to the hall Sarah nearly knocked us down, moving as fast as her little yellow legs would carry her.

"What in heaven's name is going on?" my mother asked, grabbing Sarah by the arm to keep her from running away.

"We have to find Finnie," she said, panting.

"He's coming over in an hour or so," I said.

"We have to find him," she repeated.

I telephoned Finnie's house, but Finnie wasn't there and Clarice didn't know where he was. I then phoned Joyce's house, but Joyce wasn't home either. For the next three-quarters of an hour, Sarah wouldn't talk to anyone; she just sat on the front steps waiting for Finnie to arrive. I waited outside with her, at my mother's request. Sarah was quite a high-spirited girl and scenes like this one were by no means unusual.

When Joyce's beat-up Honda pulled into the driveway, Sarah sprang from the steps, blowing frantically on the whistle attached to her life jacket. The shrill noise startled Joyce, causing her, momentarily, to forget she was driving. She remembered in the nick of time, stopping inches from the garage door.

"Sarah!" I said sharply, also startled by that damn whistle.

She ignored me and ran up to the passenger door.

"What's the matter, Sarah?" Finnie asked.

"Something bad is going to happen," she said.

"What?"

"I don't know. The lamp showed me your dad walking backward."

"Walking backward?"

"Yes, I saw him walking backward in a circle. Something bad is going to happen."

Joyce looked at me as if to ask if she was really seeing a little yellow seven-year-old girl in a life jacket standing in the driveway warning Finnie of impending doom. I shrugged. It was dangerous to dismiss Sarah out of hand; sometimes she was right.

Joyce and I followed Sarah and Finnie into the house. They went straight to the kitchen, where Finnie picked up the phone and called his father. Roger Walsh was at the sawmill, in a meeting with some raw-log suppliers. He was somewhat inconvenienced by Finnie's call and was undoubtedly even more so when he discovered that his son was calling him to see if he was okay. He said that he was fine, as far as he knew.

Somehow Sarah's fatalism had rubbed off on me; I could hear my father's voice ringing in my ears, over and over, "Bad, bad work, Mr. Starbuck."

"What's the matter with you?" Finnie asked me.

"He knows I'm right," Sarah said.

"You look pale," Joyce said.

"No, I don't."

"Yes, you do," Finnie said.

"No, I don't. There is nothing wrong with me. You talked to your dad, right, and he's fine. It was nothing, Sarah. You were wrong," I said.

Sarah shook her head. "I saw him walking backward."

"So what? That doesn't mean anything. People walk backward all the time." I walked backward around the kitchen table. "Look at me, I'm walking backward. Is something going to happen to me?"

"No. It's not the same."

"Look, Paul, let's just forget it, okay?" Finnie said, placing a hand on my shoulder.

"Yeah, sure. I'm sorry."

Sarah stood looking at the floor, her shoulders slumped. "I saw him. I'm not lying."

"I know. It'll be ok."

Sarah, never one to stay mad for long, looked up and smiled. Finnie put his hand on her head and tousled her hair. "Hey Sarah, Joyce and Paul and I are going to go to the movies this afternoon. You want to come?"

Joyce and I simultaneously looked at Finnie; we'd made no plans to go to the movies. Finnie gave us a look that said we were going.

We piled into Joyce's rusty car and set off to the theatre. Joyce and Finnie were in the front and Sarah and I were in the back. Everyone was uncomfortably quiet during the ride. I was still preoccupied with the voice in my head, Sarah was waiting for something bad to happen, Joyce was probably wondering how she had managed to get mixed up with us and God only knows what was going through Finnie's mind.

About halfway through the picture, I looked over at Finnie. He was staring blankly at the screen and his hand, perched awkwardly on the armrest, was shaking. Joyce quietly took his hand in hers and Finnie looked at her, his eyes wide with fear. She leaned over and kissed him on the cheek and then pressed his head onto her shoulder, where it remained for the rest of the movie.

On the ride home we were assaulted by a barrage of questions from Sarah about the movie. She always did this. It's not that she didn't know what was going on; she did. She just wanted to make sure she was right about what she *thought* was going on, to see if anyone else had seen something she hadn't. Normally I didn't appreciate her interrogations; I saw movies and television as a kind of escape and thought that overanalyzing their content negated that effect. I also felt stupid much of the time, still do, because I can never remember the names of characters in, or plots of, books and movies, anything at all, for more than 10 or 15 minutes. If it's real, I can remember it forever. It's good, in a way, because it keeps my head from filling up with useless crap.

Finnie, on the other hand, never forgot the slightest detail. Sometimes I wondered if he actually knew the difference between fact and fiction. I think he *did*, but often chose to ignore it.

Finnie and Joyce answered Sarah's questions the whole way home and even after they dropped us off, Sarah didn't let up. I told her I was tired, which I was, so I went to my room to lie down. I fell asleep; I don't know for how long. I awoke with a jolt when my door opened. My mother stood in the doorway.

"Paul, there's someone on the phone for you."

"Tell them I'll call them back," I said groggily.

"I think you should probably take it."

I rushed to the phone.

"Paul?" Joyce's voice came over the line.

"Joyce? What's wrong?"

"Mr. Walsh is in the hospital. He had a stroke."

"Is he okay?"

"I think so. He'll live at least. The doctors aren't saying much right now, but they think that it was a mild one."

"That's good," I said, relieved.

"There's more, though."

"There is?"

"Yes." Her voice was shaky, almost a whisper. "No one knew what was wrong with him at first. He had the stroke in his office, I guess. His secretary only realized something had happened when she saw what he was doing."

"What do you mean?"

"She went into his office when he didn't answer her on the intercom. He was pacing around his desk."

"So?"

"He was walking backward, Paul. He could only walk backward."

Across the kitchen Sarah stood very still, looking at me. I dropped the phone.

"I told you I saw it," she said. Then she scuttled over to me and wrapped her tiny yellow arms around my leg.

We never discussed the accuracy of Sarah's prediction. What was there to say about it really? Sarah knew things she shouldn't. All we could do was try not to think about it too much.

Roger Walsh recovered quickly and was soon back at work, able to walk forward or backward with equal ease. From time to time he experienced a slight numbness on the left side of his body, but other than that there were no lasting side-effects. His doctor put him on a strict diet and exercise regime, which was more of a bother than the stroke itself.

◆

The summer of 1988 passed in the blink of an eye; before we knew it Labour Day weekend had arrived. Joyce was to leave for university in a few days, so Finnie was throwing a goodbye party for her at his house. His father was on his annual fishing trip with his buddies from college, a 30-year tradition. He was determined that a mild stroke wasn't going to ruin his perfect record of attendance. I'm not sure Finnie had his permission to throw the party. I'm not even sure he needed it.

More people than expected showed up. I suppose that the prospect of a rare glance inside the house of the wealthiest family in Portsmouth outweighed any fear of Finnie's temperament. The guests' concerns were totally unjustified; Finnie proved to be the perfect host.

By the time everyone was gone, Finnie was a drunken slobbering mess. He became violently ill. Joyce and I tried to comfort him, to keep him company, but he sent each of us away, asking only to be left alone with his misery. Mercifully, he passed out and Joyce and I carried him to bed. As we were leaving the room, he mumbled something neither of us could understand. Joyce asked him to repeat himself and with great effort Finnie managed to gurgle out an intelligible sentence, "I'm going to need an eraser."

I was confused and tried to coax an explanation out of him, but none came. Joyce just shrugged and opened two fresh beers, passing one to me. We sat behind the house, on a deck that overlooked the grounds of the estate. I guess I appeared worried, because Joyce tried to reassure me that Finnie would be okay. "He'll live," she said.

"I know."

"Finnie doesn't like people to see him when he's hurt."

"No one does, I guess."

"Finnie more than most."

"Finnie feels a lot of things more than most."

"Yes, he does."

I'm not sure why I asked Joyce, but suddenly I needed an answer. "Why are you leaving?"

"Because I have to. There's no future for me here."

"Finnie's here," I said.

"Yes, but he's two years younger than me, Paul, and still has a couple of years of school left. I need an education. I need to get out of this town."

"It's not so bad."

"No, it's not. I'll probably be back someday. But I can't live here my whole life. Going away, it's my ticket, like Finnie's ticket is hockey and your ticket is. . . ." Joyce paused. She didn't know what I was going to do with my life anymore than I did. Maybe I had a shot at being a hockey player, maybe I didn't.

"I guess I understand what you're saying," I said. Portsmouth was no place for a girl like Joyce.

We sat quietly for a while drinking our beer and then she spoke again. "Hey, Paul, can I ask you a question?"

"Sure," I said.

"Why does Sarah wear that life jacket all the time?"

"Finnie never told you?"

"He wouldn't. He said I wouldn't understand."

"He might be right. I'm not sure I understand it."

"It has to do with her visions, right?"

"Yes. She thinks that she's going to drown."

"How?"

"I don't know. No one really knows."

"Not even Finnie?"

I paused. "He might. I've never asked him."

"Why not?"

"Because I don't want to know. I wish Sarah wasn't the way she is. What's she going to do, wear that life jacket her whole damned life?"

"What if she's right?"

"Then we're all fucked."

"Maybe we are anyway."

Joyce went away to McGill a couple of days later. She came back on holidays and she and Finnie spoke over the phone fairly regularly, but long-distance relationships have their reputation for good reason. Oddly enough, though, it was Finnie who gave up on the whole thing. They held on until April of 1989: eight months. When Joyce told Finnie that she would be staying in Montreal for the summer to work instead of returning to Portsmouth, he thought it best to end their relationship. He was a wreck for the rest of the summer.

◆

During the previous hockey season, 1988–89, Gretzky's first season in Los Angeles, the Great One showed that he was a commodity worth paying for, scoring 54 goals and 114 assists, a total of 168 points. In the playoffs, Gretzky and his Kings knocked out his former Edmonton Oiler teammates in the first round, rallying back from a 3-1 deficit. They were swept by the Calgary Flames in the second round.

Peter Stastny collected only 85 points that year and had the highest number of penalty minutes in his career. The Quebec Nordiques were tied for last place in the league and did not make the playoffs for the third season in a row. When Peter Stastny was traded to the New Jersey Devils during the 1989–90 season, Finnie didn't say a word. He just shook his head.

The 1988–89 season had treated Finnie and me more favourably. Finnie was once again voted team MVP and my hard work continued to pay off. Our team won the provincial championships; even Coach Hunter seemed to be happy with our performance. The 1989–90 season would be our last season of city league play, after which we could go to the WHL, which meant leaving Portsmouth. We hoped we would be drafted by an NHL team that summer; we would turn 18, making us eligible.

I didn't really know what Finnie's prospects were; Finnie was the best goalie I knew, or had ever played against, but there were a lot of good goalies out there. A WHL team would want him, but I wasn't sure if he would play in the junior leagues. He might play for an NHL farm team if he had to, but Finnie was picky and, like all goalies, a little defensive when his skills were called into question.

As for me, I was pretty sure that this would be my last season. I hadn't been approached by scouts from any of the WHL or university teams and certainly no NHL scouts had been sniffing around. Maybe I would play in a recreational league after this, a beer league. The prospect of my hockey career going no further didn't really bother me.

The night before the first game of the 1989–90 season, I had the dream again. It was the same dream I had been having every couple of months since 1981, since the day Joyce taught me how to skate. It was different this time, though, more detailed.

♦

I was in an arena, a large one. The stands were filled with screaming, cheering people. My skates were fast under my feet and my stick was weightless. A teammate passed me the puck at centre ice and I skated into the opponent's zone. Something grabbed the back of my jersey. The air around me was charged. A few of the other players stopped following the play and glided away from me; then I lost my balance and started to fall. Somehow I managed to get a shot off and as I fell to the ice I saw the goal light go on and then the crowd exploded. The players on the other team skated over to the referee, complaining about something. The players from my team skated toward me to celebrate the goal. I was in a state of euphoria, as happy as I've ever been, when I heard my father's voice echo in my head, that haunting phrase that I seemed to be unable to escape, "Bad, bad work, Mr. Starbuck." I couldn't breathe. It felt like someone was choking me, their grip firm around my throat. My arms and legs were twitching and I felt the vomit rising, but there was nothing I could do. My limbs became very heavy and the noise around me began to fade. As my vision blurred and wavered, I saw Finnie standing above me, smiling. His eyes were nearly closed, but one joyful tear rolled down his cheek. It landed squarely in the middle of my forehead, making a noise like a hammer striking tin. Then I woke up.

◆

The last year of high school flew by; we had graduated. Suddenly, we had the rest of our lives to think about. The NHL draft would take place in several days. Finnie was certain to be drafted, probably in one of the early rounds. There was a chance I could be chosen in the later rounds if I was very lucky. This was small comfort, though. Being drafted by a team and playing for it are two very different things. Even if I was drafted, odds were that I would be cut from the team at training camp and would spend the rest of my short career in the farm leagues, never even seeing NHL ice.

This didn't upset me too much. Although I would have done almost anything just to play one game for a big-league team, I was a realist first and foremost. I began to look through university calendars and brochures in an attempt to keep my options open. My grades weren't great, but they were respectable so I had a greater chance of getting into a decent school than of becoming a professional hockey player. One thing was certain; I would not be working in the Walsh sawmill.

My father had just celebrated his 50th birthday, yet he acted like an 80-year-old curmudgeon. He had become increasingly frustrated by the continuing disappearances of Mr. Palagopolis' prosthetic arms. Pal was 62 and would retire in a few years. The prospect of life without work did a lot to ease the torment of his vanishing claws, but my father, who for all intents and purposes had been retired for going on 10 years, was as antsy as ever, hot on the trail of the one-arm bandit. On several occasions my father had come close to catching his prey, but each time the one-arm bandit had eluded him by the narrowest of margins. The whole thing was absurd, really. Poor Pal was a nervous wreck half the time.

Louise was still working at the grocery store and still living at home. She had no real plans to leave and my mother appreciated her help with Sarah, a very energetic eight year old. There was something different about Louise; she was neither shy nor outgoing. It was like she was in a holding pattern.

Louise still wasn't dating, much to the disappointment of the local male population. I was often asked what was wrong with her and to tell the truth I thought, even though they didn't know it, they were dodging a bullet. Louise was definitely not what they were looking for. They rarely saw it that way, though. All they saw was a pretty face.

When people looked at Sarah, which was often, they saw a gangly, yellow child who was far too old to be constantly wearing a life jacket. My mother had tried several times to get her to take it off, but Sarah put up such a fight that my mother gave up and the life jacket stayed on. Various teachers had attempted to persuade her to remove it as well, in particular her gym teacher, who thought that it gave her an unfair advantage at dodgeball and other sports that use fear of being hit to motivate. The life jacket was, however, an ideal garment for a kid like Sarah, who was always falling down and bumping into things. Its padding protected her from bruising, which she was overly susceptible to, perhaps on account of her unusual pallor. Thankfully, Sarah hadn't had any of her premonitions since she'd seen Roger Walsh walking backward.

My mother had been working as a secretary in a law office downtown for almost 10 years now and she'd recently been promoted to the position of office manager. The promotion came with a fairly substantial pay raise, which eased our family's financial burden somewhat. It was, however, a much more demanding job, taking up more and more of my mother's time. Louise and I were fine with this; Sarah missed her, though, as did my father.

In a time when at least half of the kids I knew had parents who were divorced, my parents enjoyed what appeared to me to be an ideal relationship. They disagreed, but they didn't fight. They seemed to enjoy spending time together and both did their fair share of the work. My father had made the transition from bread-winner to homemaker without major incident and my mother had entered the workforce with equal ease. The new demands on my mother's time meant that my father only saw her for a few hours each day, if he was lucky. This was hard on him, since he'd always relied heavily on her; she was one of a very select group of people willing to put up with his peculiarities.

And, of course, just when my father was in this weakened state, the one-arm bandit struck again. Mr. Palagopolis had followed almost all of the proper procedures, but to no avail. He was overly apologetic; he knew that he wasn't supposed to remove the claw while at school, for any reason. My father forgave him this tiny indiscretion, knowing somewhere in his heart that Pal had tried his best.

My father was beaten. The one-arm bandit had won. "If I were you, Pal, I wouldn't get myself any more claws," he said.

For once in his life, Mr. Palagopolis was speechless.

♦

A week before the draft, Joyce came back to town. She was out of school for the summer and had a few days before she started her job. Although she wasn't dating Finnie anymore, she called him up. He called me and the three of us went to see a movie, then to the reservoir. Things between Joyce and Finnie were a bit tense at first, the conversation filled with terse sentences, but it didn't take long for the awkwardness to disappear. To her credit, Joyce didn't make us feel like we'd been left behind. She could have gone on and on about her two years in Montreal, all the new friends she'd made, all the things she'd learned. She could have looked down on the two of us, uneducated small-town hicks that we were. But she didn't. Good old Joyce Sweeney.

She was still driving her beat-up Honda, which had gotten progressively rustier. I was surprised when she dropped Finnie off first, though it made sense, geographically speaking. When she pulled into my driveway, she set the parking brake and turned off the engine. "So, how have you been?"

"Okay, I guess." I wondered where she was going with this; we had already had this discussion.

"I guess what I really want to know is how Finnie has been," she said.

"He's been fine. He had a tough time, when you first broke up, but he's better now."

"Is he seeing anyone?"

I hesitated. Finnie had seen a couple of girls, off and on, since his breakup with Joyce, but I didn't know if I was supposed to tell her that or not.

"It's okay, Paul. I'm not asking because I want to start anything. I just want him to move on."

"He has," I said, wondering if it was true.

"That's good."

"Yeah."

"Look, everything's fine. We both know that it's over. We're just not the right people for each other."

"Maybe not," I said.

"Right. Finnie understands that. It's just that, well, you know Finnie. He has a strange way of dealing with problems."

That much was true. In fact, it was an extreme understatement. I was still thinking about Finnie's problem-solving skills when Joyce leaned over and kissed me on the cheek. The hair on the back of my neck stood on end and my toes curled.

"You know, Paul, you're going to make a great husband one day," she said, releasing the parking brake, my cue to get out of the car. As she backed out of the driveway and drove down the street, turning left at the end of the block without signalling, I knew that I had just done something that I shouldn't have done, something very, very wrong. It wasn't the fact that she had kissed me, harmlessly and without any hint of impropriety; it was that when she had kissed me I had wanted to kiss her back. Even though she was one of my best friends and Finnie's ex-girlfriend, for whom I suspected he still had feelings, something had happened. I knew then and there that I was in trouble, real trouble. My life had just become a lot more complicated.

In the days that followed, I tried my best to push these feelings to the back of my mind, a task made easier by the upcoming NHL draft. Finnie and I killed the time any way we could — entertaining Sarah, listening to my father and Pal out on the back deck, getting drunk — anything to avoid thinking about what would happen if we weren't picked. Finally the day came and we gathered around the TV at Finnie's house. We had considered attending the draft in person, but it was somewhere in the United States that year and a long way to go. Roger Walsh had recently invested in a satellite dish, so we would be able to tune in live.

Roger Walsh was out of town on business, my mother was working, my father and Pal were at the library settling a long-standing argument about porpoises and Louise had taken Sarah to the mall. Finnie was drafted halfway through the third round, 67th overall. He went to a good team, a team with a reputation for snagging hot young goalies, and he was more than a little pleased. After the initial celebration, we settled down and waited to see if I would be as lucky. By the time the final round came, I was thoroughly convinced that I was out of the running. Finnie remained optimistic. "Nothing's over until the buzzer sounds," he said.

My heart nearly stopped when, with only three picks remaining, I heard my name called. I was even happier when I realized that the team that had picked me was the same team that had picked Finnie. Of course, being picked 256th overall meant that I was unlikely to ever play in the NHL, or even on the farm team, but it was better than nothing. I had been drafted into the NHL.

My father was so excited when I told him that he almost had a stroke. Louise and my mother were happy for me too. Sarah was not happy at all. "This means you'll be going away?" she asked.

"Yes, but I'll be back. I'll probably get cut after camp."

"That's no attitude to have, Paul," my father said. "You'll be fine."

"What about Finnie?" Louise asked.

"He'll likely get signed to the farm team, but he probably won't get to play in the NHL for a couple of years."

"Oh." She looked at the ground.

"Maybe you shouldn't go," Sarah said.

"What?" I asked.

"Well, maybe you should just stay here."

"Are you kidding?" my father said. "Paul's going to that training camp if I have to drag him there myself."

Roger Walsh was also pleased when Finnie told him he had been drafted. Of his four sons, Finnie was the only one who still had a chance at making something of himself, although both Patrick and Gerry had survived their run-ins with the law. Patrick had served only six months in a minimum-security facility that had reminded Roger more of a country club than a prison and Gerry got off with a suspended sentence. Patrick was now somewhere in Asia, on something of a spiritual quest, or so he said, and Gerry was working in Toronto as a baker's assistant. As for Kirby, he was still in jail in New Orleans, his sentence having been extended after a prison-yard altercation in which he had seriously injured a guard.

Finnie, however, seemed to be on a fast track to success, wealth and the happiness that is supposed to follow. His temper appeared to be well under control. No one knew where the Walsh boys got their tempers from; Roger had never been in a fight in his life and the late Mrs. Walsh hadn't had a mean bone in her body. Perhaps they were the product of a household without a female role model.

My father and Roger Walsh stood side by side at the airport when we left for training camp that September, each of them sporting a goofy grin. My mother had to work and wasn't able to come, but Louise and Sarah were there.

I was almost more concerned about the flight than I was about where we were going. It was the first time I had ever been on an airplane. Of course, the flight passed without incident; people who worry about plane crashes almost never die in them. Actually almost no one dies in plane crashes and if you have to die it seems to me that there are worse ways to go. What turned me off the idea at the time was the prospect of *mass* death.

Finnie didn't agree with me. He thought that if you die under these circumstances you become part of something larger, something that renders you anonymous. "It makes a bigger bang if you're anonymous," he said.

I had no idea what he meant.

Third Period

Any notions I had entertained about what training camp might be like were tossed out the first day. Even though several of the team's best players weren't there, either because of contract disputes or because they just plain thought that they didn't need to be, the skill level on the ice blew me away. Finnie felt it too; the shots were harder, the players were faster, they turned quicker, skated better and made picture-perfect passes 9 times out of 10. It was unbelievable. These were NHL players, the best in the world.

Much to my surprise, we both made the first cut. I had fully expected to be dropped from the roster at the earliest opportunity. I had even packed my bag. But when the team posted the roster my name was on it. I guess someone in the organization liked my play. Finnie had improved noticeably, his confidence growing every day. I fully expected him to make the second round.

To my disbelief, we both made it. There were two more sets of cuts to go, but whatever happened I was almost assured a spot on the minor league farm team, which was, as far as I knew, a paid position.

When the third set of cuts came, my name was on the list. The general manager told me, if I wanted, I could play in the minor league and develop my skills. In a year or two I might earn a spot on the NHL team. I signed a one-year contract for next to nothing and my professional hockey career began. It wasn't the NHL, but it was hockey and that was good enough for me.

Finnie was disappointed to see me go; he had hoped that we would both make the team. I had three weeks off before the season started, so I got on a plane and headed back to Portsmouth. Three days later Finnie showed up; he had been dropped from the roster in the fourth and final set of cuts and had been offered the same deal I had signed. He had accepted it; we would be spending the season together.

"I couldn't let you play for just any goalie," he said.

"Well, at least now you'll have decent defence."

"That's why I signed. You and me, we're a unit."

That is exactly how we played for the first half of that season. We were both at the top of our game; we had something to prove, not just to everyone else, but to ourselves. We knew that the NHL was within our grasp and given the right circumstances we could make it. That's what Finnie said anyway. Truth be told, I was pretty happy staying where I was. The play was challenging, but nothing like it had been at training camp; Wayne Gretzky and Peter Stastny don't play in the minor leagues.

When we came home for our Christmas break, Finnie's statistics were as good as those of any other minor league goalie. Mine stacked up pretty well too. I was tired; it had been a gruelling three months and the 10 days we had off were a much-needed rest. I should have known that Finnie wouldn't rest, though.

By the end of the third day back in Portsmouth, Finnie had completely rebuilt the rink. On the fourth day the ice was hard enough for skating; Finnie was there from dawn to dusk every day until Christmas. We had both become minor celebrities, so there was no shortage of people to play with at the rink, which threw me a bit. Of course, those who showed up wanted to score on the great Finnie Walsh and when they did he accepted it with class and a healthy measure of sportsmanship. The day before Christmas, he had trouble with the edge of one of his skate blades, a problem that caused him to fall easily. As a result he let in a lot of soft goals, but he didn't let it phase him. He just got right back up and stood in his crease, focusing on the next shot.

On Christmas Eve, Finnie came over to the house to visit with my family. Everyone was happy to see him, but no one was more vocal about it than Sarah. She could have raised the dead with the racket she made.

"It's Finnie!" she shrieked when he came through the door. She ran up to him and grabbed his leg.

Finnie managed to pry her off and she danced around the room in erratic circles, blowing on her whistle.

"Sarah! Stop that!" my father snapped. He hated that whistle more than the rest of us. It always startled him, causing him to drop his book, spill hot tea onto his lap or choke on a piece of toast.

My father brought Finnie a glass of his special eggnog. I have no idea what was so special about it, besides the rum, but he called it his special eggnog and no one was about to argue.

"I hear you rebuilt that old rink this year," my father said.

"Yep. It's nice to play somewhere where there isn't any pressure."

"What rink?" Sarah asked.

"Up by the reservoir," Finnie said.

"Oh. I'm not allowed to go up there."

"You're not?"

"No. Louise says it's too far."

"Well, Louise probably knows what she's talking about."

Sarah moved closer to Finnie and tried to look as cute as possible. She did this whenever she wanted something and it tended to be fairly effective. "Maybe you and Paul could take me?" she said, smiling.

"If it's okay with Louise."

Finnie knew that I had bought Sarah a pair of skates for Christmas and so did Louise. Finnie told Sarah that we'd take her on Boxing Day. That was supposed to be our last day in Portsmouth.

"You still wearing the number 13?" my father asked.

"Yes."

"How's it working for you?"

"Well," Finnie answered carefully, "I think it's working fine. I mean, it's not an *unlucky* number for me anyway."

"I think it's a good number."

"So do I."

In truth, the number had been a bit of a problem for Finnie since he had reversed it following Pelle Lindbergh's death. Whether this was just symbolic or some attempt to rewrite his own history, I'm not sure. Finnie was a collector of sorts, except that he was also a modifier. When he kept something that reminded him of a particular situation, he always seemed to change it slightly, as if to alter the actual event. When he'd changed his number from Lindbergh's 31 to Finnie's 13, he'd irreparably tied his own fate to Lindbergh's. He'd doomed himself to being Lindbergh's antithesis. I think he had already realized this on some level.

Later, after everyone else had gone to bed, or in the case of Sarah been *sent* to bed, Finnie and I went out to the garage. It was pretty much the same as it had been since my father had saved us from it years ago. My mother and Louise avoided it like the plague and Sarah thought the fish were laughing at her, mocking her with their bulging eyes. My father had been forced to set up a small portable heater next to the fish tube to keep it from freezing during winter nights and the excess heat kept the garage at a bearably warm temperature. Finnie stood, staring at the cages, playing the old game.

"Find the jumper cables," I had said, trying to give him a challenge.

Finnie stood in front of the fish tube and assessed the situation. After a while, his gaze shifted from the cages to the garage door, where it remained transfixed. When he spoke, his voice was soft. "Your dad is the reason I became a goalie."

"I know."

"I mean, we kept him awake all afternoon, making all that noise, and he didn't say anything because of my father...."

"Yeah."

"And then he gave me that rock."

I paused. My father still gave Sarah rocks sometimes. "What's the deal with the rocks anyway?"

Finnie looked at me. "You mean you don't know?"

"No."

"There is no deal. It's a smokescreen."

I still didn't understand.

Finnie looked back toward the cages. "Whenever your dad gave you a rock, what did you do?"

"I sat there and tried to figure out what the hell the rock was supposed to mean and how it had any relevance to my problem and how my father could possibly think that a rock was going to make any difference."

"Exactly. That's what you were thinking about. What you weren't thinking about was the problem."

"You mean it was all a distraction?"

"Sure. Most problems have a way of working themselves out. When the time comes, we just know what to do." Finnie continued to stare at the cages.

I just sat there absorbing what he had said.

"Joyce's in town," Finnie said.

I froze, suddenly feeling guilty. "Yeah?"

"Yep. I saw her yesterday."

"How is she?"

"Same as always."

I considered my options and for some reason I decided to be bold. "You still have feelings for her, don't you?"

Finnie looked at me and then down at the floor. "It will never work out."

"Why not?"

"It just won't. We both know it."

"You've talked about it?"

"Yes. There's nothing either of us can really do. Maybe if things were different, well, then things would be different."

"That's a lot of bullshit," I said.

Finnie shrugged. "Maybe it is. But that's the way things are."

His attention had reverted back to the cages. He was staring at one in the upper right-hand corner, mentally weighing its potential contents. Slowly he moved toward it. He reached up and opened it. His hand disappeared inside it. When it emerged, it held the jumper cables.

"Jesus, Finnie. How do you do that?"

"I don't know. It all just somehow makes sense."

◆

On Boxing Day of 1990, Finnie, Sarah, Louise and I set out to the reservoir. It would be Sarah's first time on the rink and she was more than a little eager to try out the skates I had given to her the day before. It was cold, but there hadn't been any new snow for a couple of days, so we wouldn't have to clear the ice. My mother bundled Sarah tightly against the cold, swaddling her in two sweaters, a thick winter jacket, mittens, a toque and scarf and bulky snow pants. Sarah had a heck of a time getting her life jacket on over all this, but she managed. With this added protection she seemed secure against the bumps and bruises that go along with learning to skate. We drove up to the Walsh sawmill, shut down for the week on account of the holidays, and proceeded to the reservoir on foot. Wrapped up as she was, Sarah couldn't really walk properly; she sort of waddled, like a Christmas goose. She was having trouble keeping up with us, so I slowed down and let Finnie and Louise go on ahead. It took Finnie longer to change into his gear because there was so much more of it. Besides, I had missed Sarah while I was away and hadn't spent any time alone with her since returning.

"How's school going?" I asked her.

"It's okay. Mrs. Sweeney's pretty nice."

I had forgotten that she was in Mrs. Sweeney's class. Sarah was the same age Finnie and I had been when we met. That seemed like such a long time ago.

"I was always scared of Mrs. Sweeney," I said.

"She's not scary," Sarah said. "She's just gruff."

"Gruff?"

"Yes. She's only pretending. It keeps the bad kids from trying anything."

I laughed. Sarah's evaluation made a lot of sense.

"Do you want to know a secret?" she asked me.

"Sure."

"You have to promise not to tell Dad."

"I promise." My interest was piqued. I had never known anyone to successfully keep a secret from my father.

"Pal has a new claw."

"What?"

"He got it before Halloween. He only wears it at school. Well, maybe he wears it at home. But he didn't tell Dad about it and he doesn't wear it when he comes to the house. He made me promise not to tell Dad."

"Why doesn't he want Dad to know about it?"

"Pal says that he has a big obsession."

I couldn't argue with that. When he had been hunting the one-arm bandit, my father had been driven to a singular purpose. Since he had given up the hunt, however, he had been calmer, as if some outstanding issue had finally been settled.

"Know what else? It's been two months and Pal still has the claw. He doesn't even lock it up."

"You're kidding."

Sarah looked at me very seriously. "I wouldn't joke about the one-arm bandit, Paul."

We turned the corner to witness the last thing in the entire world we would have expected. But there it was, plain as day.

"Holy shit," Sarah said.

Beside the old pump house stood Finnie and Louise. They were holding each other close and they were kissing. Like they were possessed. Either they didn't know we were watching, or they didn't care, because they sure didn't stop. I just stood there, bewildered, my jaw agape, until Sarah intervened. She inhaled as mighty a breath as her lungs could hold and blew into the whistle. The quiet was obliterated by its shriek. It scared the pants off Finnie and Louise, though thankfully not literally. Louise banged her lip on Finnie's chin, causing Finnie to bite his tongue.

"Jesus Christ, Sarah," Louise yelled. "What the hell are you doing?"

"What the hell are *you* doing?" Sarah scuttled behind me, using me as a shield.

"What does it look like?"

"Looks like you and Finnie were kissing," I said.

"Well, then, does anyone have a problem with that?" she asked.

"No," I said. For some reason I was a little frightened of Louise at that moment.

"I guess not," Sarah said. "But it's gross."

"Then that's settled. Finnie and I were kissing and no one has a problem with that, so for the love of Christ, Sarah, lay off that whistle before it kills someone."

"Sorry," Sarah said.

Finnie had remained quiet until then, perhaps because of his bitten tongue. "Anyone want to skate today?"

This sounded like a good idea to me — anything to relieve the tension. We all put on our skates and after 15 minutes the whole thing was old news. It all made perfect sense, really. Louise had been after Finnie for years, or at least since the night he'd knocked out Frank Hawthorne's eye. Even when they were kids, they always had a strange mutual understanding. It wasn't like Finnie and Joyce; there were no sparks, no magic, but Finnie and Louise just seemed like a natural fit. Getting used to the idea did not require much time. I mean, Louise was my sister and Finnie was my best friend, but even though one might think that would be awkward, it wasn't. Of course, I was young and more than a bit naïve, so I didn't understand that things that are obvious and simple are rarely easy or timeless.

As for Sarah, I don't think she much cared either way, so long as she didn't have to watch. Besides, Sarah was able to adjust to almost anything. That was one of her greatest qualities.

The first time Finnie tried to stop a shot, he fell down, sliding right out of the net and into the corner. "I don't believe it," he said.

"You fell on your ass," I said. "What's not to believe?"

"I forgot to sharpen my skate. I've totally lost the edge on this one."

"Nice going."

"Yeah. The other one's fine, though. I could shave with it, if I wanted."

"That's not going to do you a lot of good."

"No, it's not."

After that we gave up taking shots, because every time he moved too fast or shifted his weight to the dull skate, he fell. Louise and Sarah were both poor skaters, so we concentrated on teaching them. Finnie was more patient, so he taught Sarah, while I gave Louise some pointers. Unlike Sarah, Louise had been skating before, but she was out of practice. After a while her legs came back, though, and it wasn't long before she was gliding around with a fair degree of proficiency.

"Good job," I said, skating ahead of her.

"Thanks," she said. "I'm not the natural skater you are."

I remembered I hadn't been much of a skater until Joyce Sweeney had given me lessons. I felt a fresh rush of gratitude.

Louise lost her balance and fell, which elicited a look of concern from Finnie, but she was fine. She got up off the ice and resumed her tentative strides around the rink.

It had started to snow, light, fluffy flakes. Before long it was really coming down. It was about two in the afternoon and even though the sun was hidden it was still fairly bright. The trees were blanketed; several inches of snow covered the ground. There were footprints and indentations around the rink, evidence of the people who'd been there since Finnie had rebuilt it, but they were being erased and only a few metres beyond us the snow was untouched.

Finnie and Sarah were off in the far corner of the rink. A layer of snow covered the ice and hampered our ability to skate. It made it harder to control your motions; if you fell down, you slid a lot farther. They were playing tag, Finnie skating past Sarah while she tried to tag him. She seemed to be having a great time, as did Finnie, but Louise and I were tired, so we went and sat down at the far edge of the rink. Our mother had given us a thermos of hot chocolate, but it wasn't hot anymore, so we just sat there and watched them.

As Finnie skated past Sarah, she reached out and tagged him, but she lost her balance and fell. Finnie coasted past her, stopping in the centre of the rink. Sarah lay just outside the goal crease, laughing. Then her laughter stopped suddenly and she looked down at her life jacket. A mitten went up to her mouth. She looked around the rink, eyes wide. She started to scream. Louise and I stood up, thinking that she had hurt herself and had only just realized it.

Finnie skated over to her as fast as he could. It took him only seconds to reach her. As he dug his skates into the ice to stop, he slipped. Maybe it was because of his dull skate blade, maybe it was because of the snow on the ice, or maybe he just fell. He tried not to land on her, sprawling out toward the empty ice, but in an instant he was on top of Sarah, who'd stopped screaming and had closed her eyes.

From where I was standing, I couldn't see exactly what happened. Finnie could, though. He immediately clamped his hand over her throat. By the time Louise and I got to them, a thin line of red was oozing through his fingers. Sarah's eyelids fluttered and she passed out.

"We have to go for help," Finnie said, preternaturally calm. "Her throat's cut. I don't know how deep it is."

"Can we move her?" Louise asked. Her voice cracked a little.

"I don't think we should," I said.

"We have no choice. If we stay here, she'll either bleed to death or drown in her own blood."

Louise and I cringed.

Finnie took control of the situation. "Paul, go get our shoes. Louise, help me get her life jacket off."

When I got back, Sarah's life jacket was off and so were Finnie's skates. There was more blood coming through his fingers and Sarah's breathing made a sickening, gurgling sound. I helped Louise with Finnie's shoes and then we put our own shoes on.

With one hand firmly clamped over the gash in her throat, Finnie scooped Sarah up with his free arm and raised himself to his feet. He adjusted her dead weight and began to jog toward the path that led to the sawmill. Louise and I followed.

Slowly, like a train going down a hill, Finnie began to pick up speed. His jog turned into a run that turned into a long-distance, full-speed gallop. It was all I could do to keep up with him and I wasn't the one carrying Sarah. I thought Louise wouldn't be able to keep pace, but she did, just barely. By the time we reached the sawmill, we had covered ground that normally took at least 15 minutes to negotiate in less than 5 minutes.

My hands fumbled in my pockets for the car keys, but my hands were shaking so badly that I couldn't get the key into the lock. Louise took them and with steady hands she opened the doors. I got into the front seat with Louise and Finnie got into the back with Sarah.

We spoke little on the way to the hospital. Louise concentrated on driving, Finnie tried to keep his hand in place and I think I must have gone into some sort of shock. It wasn't until the next day that I even noticed that I'd sprained both my ankles on the way to the car.

When we reached the hospital, we were engulfed. Doctors swarmed around Finnie and Sarah, shouting at him not to move his hand. They were ushered through doors, but Louise and I were prohibited from following.

My parents were called, I assume, by Louise. My memory of

those hours, during which there was no clear indication that Sarah would live, is a blur. Her lungs had filled with blood, restricting her breathing, and she had lost too much to be sure she'd live.

My father, fearing the worst, said, "Sarah was from another place. She was a sentinel. She was a catalyst."

I believe that my father was right. She was a catalyst. She prompted us all to do things that we probably wouldn't have otherwise done and to think about things that without her would have gone unpondered.

♦

"She was right, you know," Finnie said, weeks after the accident.

"No, she wasn't. She said she'd drown. That's not what happened."

"You're wrong, Paul. She did drown, sort of. It was the blood in her lungs."

Right before the accident, before anyone could have possibly known what would transpire, she had screamed, as though she knew exactly what was going to happen. But this foreknowledge might even have contributed to the accident; if she hadn't screamed, Finnie wouldn't have skated toward her. Maybe he wouldn't have fallen. Maybe.

♦

Sarah pulled through, barely, flatlining twice on the operating table. There was a scar on her throat to mark the slice of Finnie's skate, a scar that would fade as she grew older but would never completely disappear. Her jugular had been nicked but not severed, which, according to the doctors, was the reason she hadn't died. That and Finnie having had the wherewithal to keep his hand locked on the wound.

There is one more thing. As Sarah recovered we realized that her pale yellow complexion, which no one had ever been able to adequately explain, had changed. She looked like a normal little girl.

◆

Near the end of January, Finnie and I returned to the minor leagues. He bought a new pair of skates, refusing to ever wear the ones he'd worn that day, but his face drained of colour every time he looked at the blades. We were shaky our first few games, making a lot of mistakes, but by the middle of February we were playing much better.

On Valentine's Day, Finnie was called up to the NHL team to back up its number-one goalie. The second-stringer had injured his shoulder in practice and would be out for two weeks. Finnie didn't get any ice time, but he practised with the team and dressed for the games. Each night there was a possibility that he might play, everyone back home tuned in, hoping to see him on the ice. I watched on nights I didn't have a game of my own and whenever the camera panned the bench there was Finnie, looking calm and collected to the untrained observer, but anyone who knew him could see that he was nervous as hell.

When the regular backup goaltender returned to the line-up and Finnie was sent back down to the minors, he played like he'd never played before. He was electric, allowing fewer goals per game than any other goalie in our league. I asked him what had changed.

"It's the big league, Paul. It's incredible."

"Why?"

Finnie hadn't talked much about his experience in the NHL since his return. "I don't know. There's something in the arenas, an excitement, almost a fever. Even when you lose a game, it's amazing. I want more. I want to play."

Finnie got his chance soon enough. He was called up again

a few weeks later and halfway through the game the coach pulled the starting goalie. The team was playing against the New Jersey Devils and Finnie let in only one goal.

"I didn't even mind," he said to me when he returned to the minors. "I mean, it's almost an *honour* to be scored on by Peter Stastny."

Finnie's performance had attracted attention from the press and was even mentioned by sportscasters on the evening news. Until then a lawyer who worked for Finnie's father had been handling Finnie's contractual affairs. Ironically enough, it was the same lawyer whom Roger Walsh had retained when the Hawthornes had sued Finnie over Frank's eye. As yet there hadn't been much work for him; both Finnie and I had the standard contract for rookies who would likely play out the balance of their contracts in the minor leagues. After his game in the NHL, however, Finnie was approached by several big-name agents. Finnie rejected their advances without hesitation. He believed that agents were a big part of what was wrong with hockey and he preferred to manage his own interests, using his lawyer to check contracts for legal snags.

Finnie was called up regularly that March, playing several more games and putting in solid performances. It seemed as though it was only a matter of time before he secured himself a regular spot on an NHL roster and, although I would miss him in the minor league, where I would certainly be spending the rest of the season, if not the rest of my career, I was happy for him. No one deserved this more than Finnie, after all he'd been through.

Things were going well with Louise as well. She visited him on the road whenever he was in a city reasonably close to Portsmouth and they talked on the phone almost every night. Finnie was determined to prevent their relationship from deteriorating the way it had with Joyce.

Louise was good for Finnie. With his popularity as a hockey player on the rise, there were many temptations open to him, temptations that might have led to trouble if he hadn't had Louise to keep him grounded.

Of course, the whole situation with Joyce Sweeney had changed since Louise appeared on the scene. I thought about it a lot and decided that if an opportunity ever presented itself I would pursue Joyce, which for me was no small resolution. Yet I didn't see her at all that spring and it wasn't long before she was pushed into the back of my mind by more pressing events.

The news came suddenly. Without any warning, Finnie was traded as part of a three-way, seven-player deal. It placed him on an NHL team that already had two top-notch young goalies, which in effect meant that the odds of him seeing any ice time almost nonexistent. He'd be sent back to the minors immediately.

This was why he'd been getting called up, to increase his marketability, a move that had been calculated by our team's management. They had been getting Finnie good press and letting him play so that he would be worth more on the trading block. It had little or nothing to do with their confidence in him or his skill as a goaltender.

"I'm meat," he said as he packed up his equipment for the last time. His flight left later that day.

"Come on, it's not so bad. Players get traded all the time."

"Yeah, I know, but I never thought it would feel like this."

"What did you think it would feel like?"

"I don't know." He paused, looking at his catching glove. "Remember when hockey was fun?"

"It's not so bad." It had been a long time since hockey had been about fun for me. I still enjoyed playing, but it was a job now; the game was not what it was when we were kids. We were being paid to play hockey. It's hard to complain about that. Besides, I wasn't very good at anything else. But I didn't love the game the way I used to.

With one month left in the season, Finnie left. With the exception of that one horrible season with Tom Kazakoff in net, after Coach Hunter had benched Finnie, and the times when he had been called up to the NHL, I had never played with another goalie. It felt unnatural for there to be someone else in his spot.

♦

Back in Portsmouth, my parents were still adjusting to the change in Sarah. One of the first things my father did was take the lamp from her room and smash it into as many pieces as he could. It was the right thing to do; my mother and Louise agreed. There was no way that the lamp could stay.

Sarah appeared to be indifferent to the lamp's destruction; she had bigger fish to fry. Before the accident she was socially outcast by other children because she was yellow and wore a life jacket and, well, was a little strange, to say the least. But now there was a whole world she wanted to see and touch and experience. Where she had asked questions before, she now answered them on her own. The only thing that bothered me was that neither hell nor high water could get her to go anywhere near a hockey rink. She wouldn't even listen to my games on the radio.

♦

A week after Finnie was traded, my call came. There was a spot open on the NHL team's roster. Three days later I would play in my first big-league game.

At first everything Finnie had told me about the NHL proved to be true. There were so many fans in the stands, all cheering and yelling, and the level of play on the ice was mind-boggling. Everywhere I looked I saw a player whom I'd seen on

TV when I was a kid. I was crashing into my heroes, taking them into the boards. They made me look like I belonged back in Portsmouth.

I was sent back down to the minors after one game. I wasn't really sure what the brass had thought of my performance. I had made some good plays, but I also knew that I had made some mistakes, so I wasn't sure if I had come out ahead.

My second game back in the minor leagues was against Finnie's new team. I wasn't sure if Finnie would be starting or not; the word was that his new team thought he had an attitude problem, which was probably true. On game day they decided that, attitude or not, he was the better of the two goalies they had, because he was there on the ice as we sang "O Canada."

Our two teams were the best in the minor league and there were several players on each team who had an ongoing feud. I didn't subscribe to that sort of thing; a game was a game and their vendettas had no bearing on how I played. In a situation like that, though, I knew it was going to be a physical 60 minutes.

There were a lot of penalties in the first period, most of them ours, but eventually our team ended up on a power play, even though we probably didn't deserve it. We had a face-off in the opposition's end. I was stationed on the right point and when the puck was dropped our centre pulled it back to me and I shot without even thinking about it. I beat Finnie high on the glove side, scoring what was the first game-situation goal I had ever scored against him. It felt so weird that I didn't even raise my stick in celebration, I just skated to the bench and sat down. When the puck had gone in, I had distinctly heard the sound of a tennis ball striking a garage door.

I guess Finnie's team interpreted my reaction to the goal as cockiness, because from then on I was a marked man. I took a number of cheap shots; some of them the referee saw and some of them he didn't. I refused to retaliate, but I delivered a number of solid, clean hits.

Early in the third period, however, I was skating to the bench on a change, not even part of the play, when a big goon of a left-winger, Eddie Johnson, came from out of nowhere and crosschecked me in the back of the head. I fell to the ice as the whistle blew. Eddie jumped on top of me and started throwing punches at my head. I was completely unable to defend myself. Johnson should have got a game misconduct, maybe even a suspension, and I should have gone to the dressing room to have my injuries attended to. But this is not what happened.

As soon as Johnson hit me, Finnie skated toward us. My team had come to my defence and a couple of guys had paired off and were sort of half-heartedly fighting or, more accurately, wrestling. The goalie on our team thought that Finnie was coming after him, so he dropped his gloves and skated out of his crease to meet him. Finnie had no intention of fighting the goalie, though. He held his stick in his hands like a scythe and swung at Johnson's head. He connected with such force that a sharp *crack* was audible throughout the arena. The acoustics of a rink are funny that way; you'd be surprised how certain sounds travel. Johnson slid to the ice, reminding me of how a building crumbles when it's imploded.

The players on both teams stopped fighting and stood, dumb-founded, not sure what to do. As far as I know, no player in the history of professional hockey has ever attacked a member of his own team during a game. Even the referee and linesmen were momentarily stunned. Finnie's coach eventually took control of the situation, scrambling onto the ice and physically removing Finnie from the building. The trainers took both Johnson and me off the ice, Johnson on a stretcher.

Johnson suffered a severe concussion and some minor neck injuries and he didn't play for the rest of the season due to what is now diagnosed as post concussion syndrome; back then they didn't have a name for it. I also had a concussion, although a far less serious one, and a swollen, bruised face. My injuries were bad enough that I missed three games.

I spent the night in the hospital for observation and in the morning, while I was waiting for the doctor to check me out, Finnie showed up. "How's the head?" he asked, smiling.

"I could ask you the same thing," I said. I still couldn't believe what he had done.

"Yeah, I guess that was a pretty stupid thing to do."

"It sure was."

"Why weren't you watching out for Ahab?"

"What?"

"That's what I thought. You should have been watching out for Ahab."

"You shouldn't have done it," I said.

"I know. I fucked up, big time. Something inside me just snapped. I don't know why."

I didn't know why either. Sarah's accident might have had something to do with it. I think that Finnie just couldn't stand to be responsible for one more bad thing happening to a member of my family or, as he saw it, a member of his family. Between Sarah and my father, he had more than enough guilt buried deep within him and he wasn't about to stand idly by and watch me get hurt. I appreciated the sentiment, but I still thought that he had over-reacted.

"What did your team say?" I asked him.

"I've been released."

"Released?"

"Yes. They said that they couldn't have a loose cannon on their team, no matter how good a goalie I was."

"But they didn't even try to trade you?"

"In their opinion I'm untradable."

"That's bullshit."

"I know. I'll get on with another team. It's just a matter of time."

"What are you going to do until then?"

"I'm going home." He turned and walked toward the door.

"Hey Finnie," I called.

"Yeah?"

"Thanks."

"Sure. You'd do the same for me."

I wasn't so sure and as a result felt a little guilty. I don't think Finnie's extreme loyalty to me was justified; I had not done anything to deserve such a sacrifice.

Finnie went back to Portsmouth the next day. News of what he'd done had travelled through the league before he'd unpacked his bags and no team was willing to give him a tryout. There are certain rules in hockey that you just can't break and most of them are unwritten. Viciously attacking a member of your own team is one of those rules and in the hockey world there were no circumstances under which such an action could be tolerated. Finnie was patient, hoping that things would blow over given a little time, but they never did. Finnie's hockey career was over

♦

The 1993–94 season was my second complete season in the NHL. I had climbed out of the minor leagues by the skin of my teeth; I had been traded four times and was a perpetual sixth defenceman, always the one closest to getting the axe. During regular-season play, I had recorded 4 goals and 10 assists, the highest totals of my career. Just before the March trading deadline, I was traded from a team that had virtually no hope of making the playoffs to a team that had a decent shot of winning the cup. I couldn't have been happier; unlike Finnie, I had no problem with being traded. Each trade was a chance to break out of my spot as the last defenceman in the line-up, a chance to prove myself. My latest trade did just that; even though I wasn't a starter, I was seeing a lot more ice time and even got in on some penalty-killing.

My new team stopped trying to use me as an offensive defenceman. I was fast, had a hard shot and could pass fairly well, which had led other teams to conclude that I would make a fairly good goal scorer if given the opportunity. But this was not the case and when I didn't score they lost confidence in me and relegated me to the bottom of the defencemen heap.

What I was, was a good, old-fashioned, stay-at-home defender, a player far more concerned with stopping goals than scoring goals. I was willing to lead a rush out of our end, but once we reached the offensive zone I was more comfortable with passing the puck to one of the forwards or at most putting a shot on net and letting someone else chase the rebound. I did not like to score goals.

This team seemed to understand these strengths and weaknesses and in the first round of the playoffs we swept our opponents. I put in a solid effort, racking up three assists in the series while preventing several goals that would have been game-breakers.

The second round of the playoffs proved to be more difficult than the first, but once again our team played up to its ability, me included, and we won four games to two. The third round proved even harder and went to seven games, with my team winning in overtime. We were on our way to the Stanley Cup finals.

♦

That year Wayne Gretzky did something that many people thought impossible. Late in March, Gretzky beat goaltender Kirk McLean, scoring his 802nd career goal, breaking Gordie Howe's 14-year record of 801. It had taken Howe 26 NHL seasons and 1,767 games to set the record; Gretzky had broken it in just 15 NHL seasons and under 1,200 games.

The year before, another record was broken. Peter Stastny's record for the most points in a season by a rookie was broken by a young Finnish player, Winnipeg's Teemu Selanne. Selanne scored 76 goals and 56 assists in his rookie year, surpassing Stastny's 109-point season by 23 points, which might not sound like a lot, but it was more points than I amassed in my entire career. Stastny only had 40 points that year and he was traded to St. Louis for the 1993–94 season, where he played only 17 games out of an 84-game schedule. The next year he would play only 6 games and would retire at the age of 39, having amassed more points during the 1980s than any other player except Gretzky.

♦

Since his involuntary exit from professional hockey, Finnie had, to say the least, deteriorated. He had become bitter, almost sarcastic, a possible result of working in his father's sawmill. Finnie had insisted that he start at the bottom of the totem pole and be treated like anyone else, regardless of who he was, and to a surprising extent that had happened. Once the guys on the mill floor got to know him, they liked him; after all, he had screwed up his life, just like many of them thought they had. He was almost one of them. The other workers could never completely forget that when he went home at night he went to the same house as the man who owned the mill, the man whom many held directly responsible for their misery. It is doubtful that Roger Walsh was responsible for anything of the sort. More the opposite; he gave them jobs — well-paying jobs — and as far as sawmills went the Walsh operation was a pretty good place to work. That's what my father had always said anyway and certainly he had ample reason to speak poorly of the lumber industry.

Roger Walsh had been against the idea of Finnie working in the mill. In principle he agreed with Finnie, but he remembered what had happened to Bob Woodward and countless others and was reluctant to expose Finnie to such a dangerous environment. Finnie seemed to have a knack for being involved in bizarre accidents. Roger Walsh shuddered whenever he thought about the possibilities created when this tendency was combined with heavy machinery.

When not working in the mill, Finnie made use of his father's satellite dish, watching as many hockey games as he could possibly fit into a day. Louise began to worry when he started yelling at the players on the screen, especially the goalies, but she didn't say anything. It was her opinion that Finnie was just going through a period of adjustment, albeit a rather long one; he would return to normal once he had worked things out in his unique way.

Finnie's weight gain was so gradual that people who saw Finnie every day hardly even noticed until one day they looked at him and saw that he weighed well over 275 pounds. This was a result of his inactivity; his job at the mill was not particularly physical and he did nothing in his free time that even remotely approached exercise. He also drank a lot more beer than he ever had before, enough to make Roger and Louise wonder if he was developing a drinking problem, although he rarely appeared to be drunk. The real problem was that there was no longer any discernible difference between a drunk Finnie and a sober Finnie. Day or night, drunk or sober, he was not himself, at least not the person we had once known.

I hadn't seen that much of him over the past few years; the NHL season was 84 games long and ran from October until April or May, depending on how long we hung on in the playoffs, which didn't leave me with much free time for visiting friends and rela-tives. I called fairly often, though, so I knew that Finnie was in a rough spot. I just didn't know what to do about it.

I wondered how long it would be before Louise left him. The Finnie she was with now was not the Finnie she had fallen in love with. He was not even a Finnie that people could really like. Louise never wavered, though. She was as true as ever and she was even suggesting, in her own subtle, languid way, that they get married. Finnie told her he'd think about it.

As for my parents, they were getting along just fine. I was able to send them money regularly, so my mother didn't have to work much. This gave her more time to spend with Sarah, who was now a typical preteen girl. One exception was her performance at school; on a standardized aptitude test, she scored through the roof. At 12 Sarah was likely smarter than I will ever be. My father was beside himself with pride.

Pal continued to be successful in concealing his secret claw from my father, who had no idea that it existed, and the one-arm bandit was equally foiled. Whether this was because of the steps Pal took to hide the claw from the general public or because the one-arm bandit had given up I'm not sure, but the result was the same. Pal kept the same claw for nearly three and a half years.

♦

The Stanley Cup final was the most gruelling hockey I have ever played. We lost the first three games of the series; going into the fourth game, we faced elimination. The mood in the dressing room was sombre; it looked like our streak was coming to an end. When we went onto the ice, however, things turned around. We won the next three games and forced a seventh and deciding game.

I decided to fly my parents and Louise out for the big night. I knew there was no way Sarah would come; she wouldn't even watch hockey on television. She hated it. That didn't bother me; I understood her reasons.

I reserved seats for the rest of my family behind our goal. For the first and third periods, they would be able to get a bird's-eye view of the action in our defensive end, which is where I spent the majority of my time. Of course, the teams switched sides after each intermission, so in the second period, and in overtime if it came to that, they would be in our offensive zone, where I rarely did my best work, but that couldn't really be helped. They arrived the morning of the game, but Finnie had come instead of Louise. She stayed home to look after Sarah.

"Wheeze thought I would enjoy the game a lot more than she would," Finnie said, grinning.

I felt like a jerk; I could easily have gotten four tickets. I had considered the idea, but had thought that Finnie wouldn't have wanted to come. After all, he was the better player. He should have been there instead of me.

The coach had scheduled a light skate that afternoon and Finnie stayed and watched while my parents unpacked. Afterward, I drove him to the hotel. I couldn't get over the difference in his physical appearance: he was grossly overweight, his hair was unkempt and he hadn't shaved in days. No one would ever have believed that he used to be a professional athlete.

"You nervous?" he asked me.

"Yeah, a bit," I said.

"You *should* be. In a couple of hours, you're going to win the Stanley Cup."

"Nothing's decided yet."

"Yes, it is. Your team will win. But I need you to do something."

"You do?"

"Yes. I need you to score a goal."

"What?"

"I need you to erase my goal. That's what started it all."

I had to think for a second before I realized he was referring to the goals he had scored against our garage door. I also knew that he was asking the impossible. "Look, Finnie, even if I could score, which is not really my role on the team, it's not going to change anything."

"I know. It won't change anything, but it will even things up. Don't worry, I'll help you."

"How?"

"There are a lot of things you know nothing about," he snapped.

As we pulled up to the curb in front of the hotel and Finnie got out of the car, he smiled. "Remember Georges Vezina?" he said.

"Sure. He went out like a pro."

"Yep. He sure did." He shut the car door.

I was just about to pull into traffic when he knocked on the window. I leaned over and rolled it down.

He stuck his head inside. "I almost forgot to tell you. Someone stole Pal's claw."

"You knew about the claw?"

"Of course I did. So did your father. He was just pretending."

"How'd he take it?"

"Your father or Pal?"

"Both, I guess."

"They both took it fine."

I pulled into traffic and was waiting at a light when I saw a beat-up, faded hockey card on the passenger seat. I picked it up; it was from the early 1930s. On the front was a balding man wearing a Montreal Canadiens sweater. He had a wide grin and bright eyes and he looked like the happiest man alive. His name was Howie Morenz. I wasn't sure why Finnie had left this card behind or even if he had done it on purpose, but I put the card into my pocket.

♦

I still had a couple of hours before I had to be at the arena, so I lay down on the bed and tried to focus my thoughts. I guess I dozed off.

It was the last time I ever had the dream and it was the clearest. As I skated past centre ice, the puck came to me and I accelerated, skating hard and fast. As I crossed the blue line, I suddenly had the feeling that something was about to hit me. I looked for someone to pass to, but there was no one open, so I shot the puck. I heard a noise that reminded me of Sarah. Something heavy and strong grabbed the back of my jersey and I fell to the ice. As I hit, I saw the puck go by the goalie, who seemed to have been unprepared for the shot. Then I heard my father's voice reverberating in my head, "Bad, bad work, Mr. Starbuck." As the players from the other team complained to the referee, I found that I couldn't breathe; something was choking me. Then I saw Finnie. He was smiling. Everything went dark.

♦

I woke up drenched in sweat. I was mad as hell. Who was Finnie to ask me to change my game, change the kind of player I was, the kind of person I was, on the day of the biggest game of my life? In the dream I was choking. In the dream I scored. But I would not change my game just because Finnie thought that it would right some sort of cosmic wrong. I died in the dream; that was, if anything, a clear sign that I should keep playing the defensive style of hockey that had gotten me into the NHL in the first place.

I knew that I did not love hockey the way Finnie did. It was just a game to me. Grown men making millions of dollars for playing a game. That's what it was, plain and simple. All the Pelle

Lindberghs and Georges Vezinas and Bill Barilkos in the world had never changed that for me. Why should Finnie? I got out of bed and drove to the rink.

The locker room was a zoo. As I started to undress, my hand unconsciously reached into my pocket and removed the Howie Morenz card. I placed it on the shelf next to my helmet. I was putting on my gear when Terry Yim, our team trainer, came by to check on me. I had been hit hard in the previous game and Terry was concerned that I might have sustained a mild concussion, but I assured him that I hadn't suffered any symptoms. He was about to leave when he saw the card up on the shelf. "Oh, wow. Where'd you get this?" he asked me.

"A friend gave it to me."

"When I was a kid, Howie Morenz was my hero. The man who died for hockey."

I was startled. I had never heard of Howie Morenz before. "The man who died for hockey?"

"Oh, sure. I guess he was a bit before your time. Morenz played for the Canadiens for 12 years, the greatest player of his generation. He was Canada's Babe Ruth. When he was on the ice, he always looked like he was having the time of his life."

I had to agree with that; the man on the card radiated pure, unadulterated joy.

"In 1934 they traded him. For the next two seasons, he played piss-poor and most people thought his career was over. Then he was traded back to Montreal. He started to play great again, until he broke his leg. Five weeks later he was dead."

"From a broken leg?"

"Oh, no. He was in the hospital recovering from his broken leg when the doctors told him he'd never be able to play hockey again. It was too much. A couple of weeks later, his heart gave out."

I was speechless. Why would Finnie have given *me* this card?

Terry rattled on, but I wasn't really listening to what he was saying until I heard a name that made my ears tingle. "What?"

"I said that Morenz played with Georges Vezina."

♦

It was a sell-out crowd that night, as all Stanley Cup games are. Eighteen thousand wildly cheering fans packed the stands. When the puck was dropped, I was on the bench. I looked into the seats to see if I could spot my parents and Finnie, but there were too many people and too many lights. I mentally reprimanded myself for doing this. I was there to play a game, not to wave at my family. I had to concentrate.

Our team scored early in the first period and then again in the middle of the period. The coach decided that the best thing we could do was to sit back and protect our lead. That was where I came in. For the rest of the first period and well into the middle of the second, I saw more ice time than I had ever seen in a game before. To my credit I was playing what was possibly the best game of my life. I broke up several plays that had the potential to score goals and when one of our guys got sent to the box I was put out on the penalty-killing unit.

Midway through the second period, however, we got caught on a bad line change and gave up a three-on-one that resulted in a goal. Now that the score was 2-1 for us, the coach thought that we should assume a more aggressive posture and I spent more time on the bench in favour of an offensively minded defenceman.

Both teams went without scoring until late in the third period, when we let in a weak shot from the point. The horn sounded and the period ended with the game tied.

As I sat on the bench waiting for overtime to begin, I looked again into the stands and this time I successfully located Finnie and my parents. They were seated behind the opposition's goal, about

15 rows up. My mother was reading through her program, no doubt checking the write-up about me to make sure that there were no mistakes. My father was wearing his Portsmouth Jaguars foam finger, which I thought would bother Finnie, but when I examined him closely he seemed to be quite calm, almost peaceful. He was so obese he could barely fit into his seat and even though he was at the seventh game of a Stanley Cup final, with the game going into overtime, his face was serene and collected.

Whatever thoughts I had entertained before the game about hockey or Finnie or the dream had vanished from my mind. All I cared about was the game and not losing it. I didn't care about winning, I cared about not losing; somehow there was a difference.

The puck was dropped and for the first several minutes of overtime both teams held back, being careful not to make any mistakes in their own zone. Then, about five minutes in, the play started to open up as the players' focus shifted to scoring the goal that would win the cup. The entire year, over 100 games, the whole championship, it all came down to one goal. It was a goal of incomprehensible proportion.

It was my third or fourth shift of overtime, about seven minutes in. I got the puck behind our net and passed it to the other defenceman. I skated out of our zone and as I reached centre ice I got a return pass. I evaded what would have been a punishing check and decided to take the puck into the offensive zone.

As I crossed the blue line, I felt a presence behind me and without looking I knew that someone was there. Ahab was there. I looked for someone to pass to, but there was no one; our other defenceman hadn't entered the zone, so a pass to him would have put us offside, and the forwards were covered. I decided to put a shot on net and hoped that someone from our team could get to the rebound. As I brought my stick back to make the shot, I was grabbed from behind. A hand, with fingers that felt like steel, like a claw, pulled me back and then pushed me forward. As I fell to the ice, I managed to connect with the puck. The shot left my stick and sailed through the air. Somewhere, in the back of my mind, I heard a whistling sound and I was reminded of Sarah. The puck flew past the goalie, who was looking in the direction of the referee. The mesh at the back of the net rippled and the red light went on. The goalie frantically skated over to the referee, complaining that the whistle had gone, that play had been halted. The referee hadn't stopped the play, however, and neither had the linesmen. None of them had heard a whistle, so the goal stood. We had won the Stanley Cup.

My teammates pulled me up from the ice and engulfed me into their mass, celebrating my goal. Gradually the reality of what had happened sank in. I had scored the winning goal. I had won the game. I had done what Finnie had asked of me. I had erased his goal.

We were presented with the cup and my teammates paraded it around the rink, which was suddenly full of reporters and officials and people who had managed to get past security and onto the ice. When the cup was passed to me, I skated over to where my parents and Finnie were sitting, but there were so many people that I couldn't find them.

It was then that I heard my father's voice. Above the roar of the crowd and my teammates howling, it rang out loud and clear, "Bad, bad work, Mr. Starbuck."

♦

Throughout the game Finnie had remained silent, calm, just like the Chicoutimi Cucumber, Georges Vezina. My father said that he never took his eyes off me. He held his left hand, his glove hand, in a fist, clutching something small and fragile. Whenever I got the puck, he would raise the fist to his mouth.

Then, finally, seven minutes into overtime, he saw his chance. As I shot the puck, he raised his fist to his mouth and blew as hard as he could. My parents were both so startled that they didn't even see the puck go into the net. They'd heard a noise that they hadn't heard in three and a half years, a noise that they'd never expected to hear again.

When they looked at Finnie, however, they saw that something was wrong. He was choking, his massive frame shuddering and his meaty fingers grasping his throat. My father tried to give him the Heimlich manoeuvre, but he only had one arm. My mother tried too, but Finnie was just too fat; she couldn't get her arms around him. The crowd around them had erupted and there was no way they could go for help. It takes a surprisingly long time for a person to choke to death. Finnie just slumped into his seat and closed his eyes. My father said he wasn't even trying to fight it, like he was just waiting for the end. When Finnie finally lost consciousness, my father was able to lower him to the ground and peer down his throat. He couldn't see anything at first, but my mother did a chest compression, just below the sternum, and, even though Finnie was already dead, his corpse reacted reflexively and spit out the object that had been blocking his windpipe. My father wordlessly reached out and put the plastic whistle from Sarah's life jacket into his coat pocket.

There were three things of interest on his person besides the whistle. In his pants pocket was the one and only rock that my father had given to him so many years ago; a partially burnt hockey card, the card of his one-time idol, number 31, Pelle Lindbergh; and a worn, crumpled picture of Georges Vezina.

Overtime

After Finnie's death, the mystery of the one-arm bandit was revealed. It all made perfect sense in hindsight. Maybe all things make perfect sense in hindsight. All the thefts took place at school. They started after my father lost his arm and ended when Finnie and I went away to the junior team. The one-arm bandit had to have inside information about my father's plans; he was always in the right place at the right time. Besides, Finnie was the only other person who knew the combination of my old bike lock.

On the morning of Finnie's funeral, there was a knock on our door. When my father answered it, he was greeted by a delivery truck driver bearing three large boxes addressed to Mr. Palagopolis, care of my father. My father signed for them and Sarah and I helped him to move them into the kitchen. He opened the first one and his jaw dropped. He didn't need to open the second or third box. When I looked, my jaw dropped too. I ripped open the other two boxes, unable to contain my amazement. Within the boxes were 25 prosthetic arms, the exact number of arms that the one-arm bandit had stolen from Mr. Palagopolis. Each claw had a sticker on it and on each sticker in red marker was written the date the claw had been stolen.

There was a note in one of the boxes, addressed to "Bob and Pal." It read, simply, "Here are the arms back. You don't need them anymore. Love, Finnie."

I was furious. To think that it was Finnie the whole time, that he was the thief who'd caused my father and Pal so much misery. "That fucking bastard," I said under my breath.

"Shut up, Paul," Sarah said.

My father laughed, making me angrier. "How can you laugh?"

"Because he's right. We don't need them anymore. He's given us that."

It took me a long time to understand what my father was talking about. It was only when I remembered something Finnie had once said to me that it began to make sense.

"Everyone's missing something, Paul," he'd said. "If you try to put something else in its place, you're only going to cause more damage."

Sarah smiled; she'd known all along what Finnie was up to.

Finnie took away my father's arm and then he took away Mr. Palagopolis's arms, but as the one-arm bandit he gave them something else in return. My father had long ago stopped absent-mindedly gesturing with his missing arm and Pal had stopped believing that his claw was out to get him. I suppose, in a sense, Finnie, the one-arm bandit, had healed them.

♦

Hockey is unique in that it is the only professional sport in which the players get to take the trophy home with them. In all other sports, the championship trophy sits in a display case somewhere, but the Stanley Cup is on the road all summer, spending two days at the home of each member of the team who won the right to possess it.

The first day the Stanley Cup sat in my parents' living room, scores of neighbours came by to see it up close and to congratulate me on the win. They all said how sorry they were about Finnie. Of course, they didn't know what had actually happened; they'd been told that Finnie had died of a heart attack.

On the second day, Louise and I took the cup up to the reservoir and placed it in the spot where the crease would have been. We sat, wordlessly, for most of the afternoon. Eventually, though, I had to ask Louise the one question that, to this day, I don't know the definitive answer to. "Do you think he meant to die?"

Louise thought for a long time before she answered. "I don't know if he *meant* to or not. But I think he knew he would."

"I had a dream, Louise. I've been having it for years."

She was not surprised. "There was nothing any of us could have done."

When they took Finnie away, strapped to a stretcher even though he was dead, there was a smile on his face.

I never played professional hockey again. I was only 22 when I retired and people thought I was crazy to walk away from what would have been a multimillion-dollar career, but there was plenty that they didn't know. I had done what I'd had to do and it was time to get out, before the game became a business and I erased the mark that Finnie had made.

I finally understood what Finnie had been saying all along, the point he'd tried to make with the Howie Morenz card. To stay in hockey, I would have had to love the game the way Finnie had loved it. I refused to be one of the people who was ruining the sport. If you don't love it, if you can exist without it, then you shouldn't be there. I had no choice but to leave. I had worn Bill Barilko's number and I would not disgrace it by staying.

I don't regret quitting hockey. Roger Walsh gave me a job, a good job, and together we have kept his business going. None of his other sons ever amounted to anything; Kirby's still in jail, this time for the rest of his life, and Patrick and Gerry are content to live on the money their father gives them each month. When Roger Walsh dies, he will leave me the bulk of his business, with the understanding that I continue to send his surviving sons money. I have grown fond of old Roger; together we have learned many things about Finnie that neither of us would have known on our own. It seems that everyone who ever came into contact with Finnie got a tiny piece of his puzzle.

Louise has never married. She maintains that she will never meet anyone who can make her feel the way that Finnie did. I wish I could argue with her, but I can't. Besides, Louise always did just fine on her own.

My mother has retired and she and my father have been travelling, seeing all those things that, until recently, my father has only read about in magazines. My father misses Pal, who died several years ago at a ripe old age. His will stipulated that he be buried with his claw.

After graduating from high school with the highest marks in the province, Sarah could have attended the university of her choice. Instead she sat down and read every *National Geographic* ever published from cover to cover. Then, perhaps inspired by the string of bizarre accidents that has plagued our family, she became a doctor. I think she's a good one too, although I have no way of knowing.

When I saw Joyce Sweeney at the hardware store a year after Finnie's death, I asked her to dinner. She hadn't been at Finnie's funeral; she said it would have been too hard. She had been living in Portsmouth for three weeks before I saw her, having decided that larger cities, while interesting, were not the sort of place she wanted to spend the rest of her life. I agree with her. We will probably live here until we die. It will take us that long to pay off our mortgage.

When I try to think of what life might have been like without Finnie, well, I can't even imagine it. Almost everything Finnie did seemed to be either fantastic or horrible and the same event had a way of being one way one day and another the next. He took us places using roads that didn't lead to where we were going.

At the end of the 1998–99 season, Wayne Gretzky retired after 21 years of professional hockey. Many think that the records he set will never be broken. The league retired his number and as his banner was raised the announcer's voice broke and a sob escaped.

A while after Finnie's death, I sat down and read *Moby Dick* in an attempt to figure out Ahab and Mr. Starbuck and that damn whale. I'm not quite sure what to make of it. Maybe Finnie was Captain Ahab, a madman obsessed with a singular purpose, a purpose that brought him to his own demise. Or maybe he was Starbuck, brought to his unfortunate end by the folly of others. Whatever Finnie Walsh was, I would give anything not to have been Ishmael.

Acknowledgments

Thanks to the faculty, students and alumni of the UBC Creative Writing Program, Carolyn Swayze, Joy Gugeler, the Galloway, Tayler and Haslett families, Chad Hunt, Lynda Milham and Helen's Grill. Special thanks to Lara, whose love, tolerance and support enabled the writing of this book.

STEVEN GALLOWAY is the author of three novels: *Finnie Walsh*, *Ascension*, and *The Cellist of Sarajevo*. His work has been translated into over twenty languages and optioned for film. He teaches creative writing at UBC and SFU, and he lives with his wife and two daughters in New Westminster, BC.